HUNGER

JANE THORNTON TRILOGY: 1

C.E. BLACK

This is a work of fiction. Names, characters, places, and incidents either are the product of the author's imagination or are used fictitiously. Any resemblance to actual persons, living or dead, business establishments, events or locales is entirely coincidental.

HUNGER

For information: authorceblack@ceblack.org

ISBN: 978-0-9987885-0-0

Printed in the United States of America

JANE THORNTON TRILOGY
BY C.E. BLACK

"There's safety in pairs, but three is better."

HUNGER
STARVED
SATED

1

"Do you see her?"

Sucking in a breath, I held it as I stared at the pair of dirty tan work boots that stopped only inches from my face. They stepped sideways as the owner turned in a circle.

My heart beat erratically, and my head swam from lack of oxygen. *Please say no, please say no,* I chanted over and over in my head.

Another pair of boots, these black, military like appeared next to the others, and I had to swallow a gasp of air. "No," another man said, his voice more of a grunt than anything.

Instead of sighing with relief, I let out my breath slow and even. I couldn't afford to make a sound. From the tone of the second man's voice, deep and unforgiving, I wouldn't like it if they found me.

I'd spotted the two men a few days before. They were walking down the center of a two-lane road, out in the open, where anyone could see them. One tall and built like a linebacker, the other not as tall, but just as big. Just as muscular. Just as dangerous.

At first, I'd been so surprised to see actual living human beings, I'd frozen. The shorter man had laughed at something the other had said, though his friend only grimaced. Whatever the joke, it must not have been too funny. Still, the sound had carried on the wind to where I stood only a few feet away. My lips had tugged up into something akin to a smile. I hadn't smiled or laughed in so long, I wasn't sure I still knew how.

However, the moment was short-lived. A glint of light had caught my attention and my eyes followed to the gun strapped on the taller man's belt. Yes, we lived in a world where guns were most definitely needed. I'd have had one myself if I hadn't run out of bullets weeks before. But I didn't trust people... Didn't trust men... Especially men with guns.

I'd seen with my own eyes what had happened when the world went nuts. Murder and rape... Out in the open, and no one stopped them. I saw it all from a tiny window in my basement. Where I'd stayed until there were no more people.

Ducking out of sight, I'd waddled down the center of a ditch until I came to a drainage pipe. Having been there before, I knew where it led and thought nothing of crawling inside. I followed the small stream of water to the other side and ran.

I thought I'd hidden in time. Thought they were just passing through and had never noticed me. I'd been wrong.

Every once in a while, I'd catch a glimpse of them, and before long realized it was me they were searching for. Sometimes, I'd catch one of their voices, asking the other if they'd seen *the girl*. I was the only girl here. The only living soul in this whole damn town. It had been almost a year since the beginning of the end, and I'd been here the entire time. It was my hometown, where I'd grown up. And where I thought I would die. Eventually. But I wasn't ready. Not yet.

I'd believed they would get tired of searching and move on. No such luck. They weren't going to give up. And if they weren't going to leave, then I had to.

"I saw her run behind that trailer. Where could she have gone?" The lower tone of the man's voice was soft, almost, but not quite a whisper.

The other grunted again. "I don't know. Maybe she ran off into woods."

"We would have seen her."

A spider crawled across the top of my hand, tickling the skin. I had to get out of there. The cool dirt beneath me caused my body to tremble with chills. And though I wasn't afraid of spiders or bugs, getting bit could cause me to itch. Between the shivers and the itching, I'd give myself up in a heartbeat.

"If she were smart, she'd be inside one of these, warming up."

"You're right. Let's check one out."

As the boots moved out of sight, I stretched my neck, keeping an eye on my stalkers. They continued straight to the mobile home in front of this one. It was the best chance I was going to get.

Using my forearms, I wiggled backwards until my legs reached the open air. I'd only gotten halfway out when the sickening sound of chattering teeth caused me to still. But only for a second. I scrambled to get back under the trailer and hadn't been quick enough.

Cold, hard fingers clamped down just above my ankle and yanked. I dug my nails into the dirt and kicked out, hoping it would be enough to keep those clicking teeth from reaching my flesh.

This was it. I would die. Or worse yet, become one of them.

No! *No giving up. Not, yet, Jane.*

Gritting my teeth, I kicked it again. Its grip loosened. But not enough. It held on tight, nails digging into my flesh as I pulled with all my strength. I did everything in my power to keep my leg away from its teeth.

I flipped onto my back, twisting my legs crisscross, the position giving me more flexibility. Yet the sight of the hideous creature's snapping teeth so close to my skin had me hesitating in horror. I jerked back as his mouth descended. That hesitation had cost me. The thing was able to drag me farther out from under the trailer. I struggled to crawl backward once again, but my strength waned. It had been so long since I'd had to fight one, I'd forgotten just how strong they could be.

The tug of war continued, and as I pulled back one more time, I reached for the knife strapped to my leg. It would be impossible to stab the flesh eater from my position. But if I wiggled just enough to pull him closer…

The grip on my leg was ripped away as the flesh eater disappeared. I leaned up, my scalp prickling with unease. I pulled my legs under the trailer and listened, hearing nothing but my own heart pounding.

The cool dirt met my chest as I ducked down enough to see out. More dirt, grass, a dead flesh eater with its brains decorating the ground, and two sets of boots. I gasped, and got up on my hands and knees, ready to make a run for it. My heart racing, I began crawling backward, as slow and soundless as I could.

"Come on out."

Ice slid down my spine, and I froze.

"We just want to help. You can't stay under there forever."

My lips pressed together. *Want to bet?*

After a deep grunt, the different voice whispered, "Shut it, Kaden." Then louder, he said, "Come on, sweetheart. We need to get somewhere safe."

I looked to my left. If I crawled out that way, would I have enough time to run before they noticed?

A gasp escaped my lips when a cold hand settled on my ankle. Then a face appeared up under the trailer. Warm brown eyes met mine. "Hi," he said. "We won't hurt you. Promise." He smiled, and it was a charming smile, a nice smile. A smile that said, *trust me.* I couldn't, though. I couldn't trust anyone.

Tugging my leg did no good. He held on. Not tight, but enough to let me know he wasn't going anywhere.

Heart in my throat, I nodded and started crawling out behind him. My gaze landed on those boots, both pairs, and I shivered. I flicked a glance at the dead thing next to them and the shiver turned almost violent. I had a feeling I might have been better off with the flesh eater. The living could be much more dangerous.

"Here you go," the brown eyed man said as he grasped my arm to help me stand.

Clutching the strap of my bag to my shoulder, I looked at the two men who'd followed me. The one who'd spoken, the brown eyed guy, smiled his nice smile again. He had a couple of days' worth of growth on his chin and cheeks, brown, like his eyes and his shaggy hair. He was maybe three or four inches taller than me and twice as wide. Not an ounce of a fat, though. He was all muscle, broad shoulders, and chest that narrowed down into thinner hips. Still wider than mine. Over the course of the last few months, I'd lost so much weight, I'd become nothing but skin and bones. I tried not to starve myself, but I had to ration my supplies. He looked like he'd been eating well, and taking care of himself if that white smile was any indication.

"Hi, I'm Mason," he said as he held out a hand. "But you can call me Mace. Everyone does."

I looked at it, then back at his face as I hitched my bag higher on my shoulder. When I didn't respond, or give him my own hand, his smile wilted. I kind of hated that. But not enough to touch him.

He dropped his hand and cleared his throat. "This is Kaden," he gestured to the other guy I hadn't yet even glanced at. And boy when I did, I wished I hadn't. I'd thought Mason was big. He had nothing on Kaden. The guy stood another five inches or so taller than Mason, and just as broad. Tilting my head to get a good look at his face was a bad idea. As I took a step backward, his scowl deepened and his blue eyes narrowed.

"Stop scaring her, Kaden—"

Before Mason could finish his sentence, I took off. A curse sounded behind me as I pumped my legs as hard as I could. My breathing was already ragged from my ordeal under the trailer, and my backpack weighed a ton. I almost threw it off to gain more speed, but my life was in that pack.

As my shoulders slumped, I thought, the hell with it! I yanked off the damn bag, letting it tumble behind me. If I could just reach the trees, I'd be safe. If there was one thing I was good at, it was hiding.

My legs flew across the grass as I forced a burst of

speed from my tired body. Close now. Only maybe a yard away.

My knees buckled and I came crashing down, face first onto the grass. I scrambled to get back on my feet, but before I could stand, I was crushed flat. I'd been caught.

The man on top of me grunted, his hot breath blowing across my neck. Laying on my stomach made maneuvering impossible. I wiggled, using my shoulders to push him. He only groaned and put more of his weight on me until no matter how hard I tried, I couldn't move a muscle.

"Be still," he grumbled.

Sitting up, he flipped me over onto my back. Eyes wide, I stared up at my captor with pursed lips, my emotions jumping from fear to anger and back again. The fine lines around his mouth and eyes tightened the longer he stared at me. I held my ground, narrowing my own eyes right back at him.

Then the realization that a man straddled my waist sent a cold chill down my spine. Swinging my arms, I aimed to punch him in the face, but I was no match for him. With hands that were twice as big as mine, he captured my wrists, pinning them to the ground on either side of my head. The move brought his face inches away from mine, causing me to tense.

"Mace said we wouldn't hurt you," he grunted.

When I didn't reply, his eyes tightened into narrow slits. Then he sighed and looked away as Mason jogged toward us.

Without the intensity of his eyes on me it was easier to look at him. He had a square jaw that jumped when he ground his teeth together. Like he was doing now. And his nose wasn't too straight. It had a small bump in the center.

His face was lean with high cheekbones that I could see even though he wasn't smiling. I got the impression he didn't smile often.

Feeling my eyes on him, his gaze flickered back to mine. When I looked away, he grumbled something under his breath. Then he shifted on top of me. The move caused his arousal to press against my belly. Panic clawed up my throat and I jerked against his hold.

He cursed under his breath and pressed down on my wrists. It took a moment for me to register that, though he could have, he wasn't causing me any pain.

"Ignore it. I am," he ground out through clenched teeth.

Ignore it? How could I?

He pulled his hips back, but the memory of his thick length seared into my brain. I refused to be played with like some freaking sex doll they found in the midst of a world where living females were rare. But I'd gone a long time without physical or emotional intimacy. I couldn't help but appreciate the stunning man above me. He and his friend could have been plucked right out of any one of my wet dreams. Good thing I'd never let my hormones rule over my brain cells, or I would have been in big trouble.

Bringing his nose almost touching distance from mine, he stared at me, his gaze intent. "We will not hurt you. Trust us."

Easy for him to say. He was the one holding me down.

"Kaden!" Mason said as he approached. "Get off of her."

Kaden stared into my eyes for a split second. Then he let go of my wrists and stood, his expression daring me to run again.

I rolled over to stand and saw Mason's hand dangling in front of me. "Here, let me help——" I batted his hand away, cutting him off as I stood on my own.

"Fine, here," he said as he handed me my pack.

Yanking it out of his hand, I slipped it over my shoulders. He handed Kaden his rifle back. He must have dropped it to chase after me.

I looked back and forth between the men. They stood on either side of me, blocking my route to the trees. *Now what?*

"I'm sorry we scared you." Mason ran a hand through his messy hair and blew out a breath. "We didn't mean for that to happen. We haven't run across anyone in so long, we just wanted to talk to you, see that you were okay. How long have you been out here alone? You shouldn't be. It's safer in pairs. Three's better, though. Think of how safe you'd be with us."

I cast a furtive glance at Kaden while his attention was solely on our surroundings. A gust of wind blew through his hair, sending a few dirty blond strands falling over his forehead. Mason continued to talk, but I had no clue what about. I'd stopped listening as I took stock of them both. Mason's expression was the complete opposite of Kaden's. Animated and with a slight tinge of pink on his cheeks, Mason's hands gestured as he spoke. Clearly the social one of the two.

Kaden never stopped frowning as he gripped his rifle, barrel pointed up. Both men had plenty of weapons. I counted at least three knives each, a couple of handguns, and the rifle. Each also had a backpack. These men weren't playing. I couldn't blame them. Times were tough.

"So, are you hungry? We have a little food," Mason was saying, just as my ears picked up the sharp chattering sound. At the same time, I saw Kaden stiffen. "We have to go," he snapped,

He reached for my arm but I yanked it back as I turned to see what he had. A group of flesh eaters, at least a dozen, were heading straight for us, their hands reaching out, ready to grab the nearest thing to feed on.

"Come on," Mason said.

He grabbed my arm right above the elbow and dragged me toward the trees I'd just been chasing after. I went with them. Nothing else I could do. There was no way I could fight off so many flesh eaters on my own.

As soon as we started running, Mason took the lead as Kaden hung back, leaving me in the middle of our little group. A means to keep me from running off, no doubt. Lucky for them, I was too pumped with adrenaline to care about that right now. The flesh eaters didn't have much speed, but it was amazing how fast they were when they got right up on you. The further away we got, the better. Yet as we scrambled uphill through dense woods, I thought of nothing but my escape.

2

———

THE THREE OF US EVENTUALLY CAME ACROSS ONE OF those packed, cookie-cutter-house neighborhoods. I'd been through this one before and it looked just as desolate as the last time I'd been there. A mixture of trash and kids' toys littered the lawns along with a few dead bodies. Seeing the dead had become such the norm that it didn't even bother me anymore. Not much anyway. I averted my eyes from the worst ones while still keeping a watch on my surroundings as the men led me to one of the houses.

"Stay here," Kaden ordered before stalking around the back of the house, leaving me alone with his sidekick.

Mason smiled, the one that said he was ready to talk. Again. After only a day, I already knew his tells. Holding back an eye roll, I leaned against the porch railing with my arms crossed, bracing myself for the onslaught of chatter about to ensue. Though I wasn't sure how much more he had to talk about. I was pretty sure he'd given me his and Kaden's whole life story already.

Kaden and Mason met in college, a lifetime ago, he'd said, but fell out of touch when Kaden joined the military.

Mason got recruited into the NFL. I looked him up and down from lowered lashes. Yep, definitely a football player. He'd never said what position he'd played, and I wasn't into the game myself so I couldn't guess, but he had that solid look about him. And Kaden screamed military, so that wasn't a surprise.

According to Mason, Kaden had called him right away when he'd learned what was happening. He'd warned him to get somewhere safe. Instead, Mason drove from Tennessee to Fort Hamilton to get his friend. Now, they were headed back to Tennessee, where Mason had some land or something. I wasn't clear on that part. After a while, I'd zoned out.

The sun dipped below the tree line, sending blinding orange light into my eyes. Squinting, I looked away, careful not to make eye contact with Mason. I had no desire to converse with the man. Though I doubted he cared all that much. My fingers curled inside my palms. Even if I wanted to talk to him—which I didn't—I couldn't. Being born mute had its advantages, I supposed. And here I thought my silence was only good for hiding from flesh eaters and evil men.

He cleared his throat, then made a scraping sound with his shoe against the concrete pathway before I heard his footsteps taking him in the opposite direction.

I watched him in my peripheral vision, surprised he hadn't started another one-sided conversation. The man sure knew how to talk someone's ear off. Instead, he faced away from me, his hand rubbing the back of his neck as he stared down at his feet.

My brows furrowed as I watched him. Had he been hurt by that flesh eater? I gave myself a mental shake and slumped back against the railing. Why was I worried over a strange man who had pretty much kidnapped me? He deserved a little pain. Maybe he hurt so much he wouldn't be able to catch me the next time I took off.

I straightened my shoulders, my arms slowly dropping to my sides. This was my chance, I realized. Excitement had me wanting to bounce on the balls of my feet, but I held completely still, keeping my focus on Mason. While Kaden was inside and Mason's attention otherwise occupied, I'd get a decent head start. By the time they caught up, they wouldn't be able to find me. Except for my last disastrous attempt, I was pretty damn good at hiding. I had to be in this world.

My eyes burned into Mason's back as I took a hesitant step away from the porch. Then another more confident step, then another. I was just about to make a run for it when the creak of the front door alerted me that Mason and I were no longer alone. A scowling Kaden stepped out of the house, his knowing eyes taking in the scene. First, he glanced at Mason, standing several feet away, his back to us. Then that impenetrable gaze landed on me, his eyes narrowing on my position. One foot out, my body leaned the same way, ready to run. I swallowed hard and slowly stood upright, crossing my arms with a sigh.

Kaden's eyes turned into narrow slits before giving a single nod to the inside of the house. "All clear."

And there went my chance.

Why did you hesitate, Jane? I gave myself a mental shake for being so stupid. Next time—yes, there would definitely be a next time—I would run. No hesitation. And I wouldn't look back.

I matched Kaden's glare, refusing to be intimidated by his muscles, good looks, or his scowl. *Good looks? Where had that come from?*

He frowned, his brows lowering as he tried to get a read on me. *Dream on*, I thought.

"This will do," Mason said as he followed me inside. Kaden had stayed by the door, his eyes glued to me as I crossed the threshold. I pretended my heart didn't flutter like a damn hummingbird's wings. I also pretended not to notice his enticing masculine scent. It called for me to lean in, bury my nose into his neck, and take a deep drag. My lips parted. From now on, I would be breathing through my mouth.

———

As night fell, the interior of the house became dimmer and darker. While Kaden made sure all the windows were covered, Mason gathered an armful of candles, setting them in the center of the room before lighting them. I'd watched as they'd unpacked, impressed with how much stuff they'd been able to put inside each bag.

I'd pulled out my one blanket. It was a wedding ring quilt, off white with vines of little burgundy flowers and deep green leaves inside the rings. It looked a little worse for wear, the edges stained and one corner had ripped. But it was warm. In more ways than one.

I wrapped the quilt around me, taking a moment to bury my nose in the fabric. It didn't smell like anything, but the comfort it gave relaxed my tired muscles. The blanket wasn't a personal heirloom. Wasn't mine at all. I'd found it while scavenging for food. But I loved it all the same.

Sitting back against the wall where I'd taken residence against the far corner of the room, I pulled the quilt over my front and watched the men as they set up for the night.

They had their sleeping bags laid out, Mason's in the center of the room, while Kaden put his closer to the front door. Neither were laying on them, though. Instead, they both were still quietly moving around the house. Searching for supplies, I assumed. They wouldn't find much. I'd been through this neighborhood, and all the good stuff had already been taken.

"Hey," Mason said as he moved toward me. The grip I had on the knife beneath the blanket tightened. He must have seen the tension enter my shoulders because he stopped a couple of feet away, and with a hesitant smile, knelt down on the balls of his feet. "You need to eat," he said.

My eyes fell on the can of food he held out. My mouth watered. I hadn't eaten all day. Still, a part of me wanted to refuse him.

I started to shake my head no when my stomach decided that was the moment to speak up, letting out a growl so loud Kaden turned to look at me from across the room. Mason chuckled and my cheeks heated.

"Go on, take the food," he insisted.

Nodding my thanks, I pulled my free hand from under the blanket and took the can from him. As I stared down at the gelatinous orange sauce covered pasta, Mason held out his hand again, this time holding a fork. "Here, you'll need this."

Setting the can on the floor next to me, I took the offered utensil with another nod. Mason glanced down at the blanket where my other hand hid underneath. He didn't say anything, but his gaze flickered to mine and gave a single sharp nod before standing up and backing up a step.

"Eat up, then we should get some sleep."

He walked away and sat down next to Kaden to eat their own dinner. Though instead of them each having a can like I did, they shared one. As I took a bite, my eyes never strayed from them. They took turns. One would take a bite, then the other. And in seconds, the can was empty. Both stared at it before sitting down their forks.

Mason cleared his throat. "We need to find more food," he whispered. His eyes shifted toward me but only for a second before he looked back at his friend. "She needs more. Hell, we all do. I can't keep going like this."

"I know," Kaden said softly. "I've searched this entire neighborhood. There's nothing left. We need to move on."

"Yeah. Think we can convince her to come with us?"

Kaden's gaze met mine and held. I looked down at my can and took another bite of pasta. "She might. Think it's still there? And empty?"

"Yeah, it's in the middle of nowhere," he replied. "I seriously doubt anyone has found it. Uncle Jay had the place set up like a dream. A well, generator, and garden already started. It'll be perfect. Plus, if I remember correctly, it's also easy to defend."

"Guess we'll find out," Kaden said.

"Yeah," Mason sighed. "We still have a way to go, though.

As they continued to talk about their plans, I thought about the food issue. They were right. There was nothing useful left in this neighborhood. I'd raided most of the town myself. And I didn't have much on me. But... I glanced at the empty can sitting between them, then back at my half-eaten dinner. I wasn't used to eating so much, and I couldn't see a reason for eating the rest when I didn't need to.

I felt the weight of their gazes as I got to my feet and

made my way toward them. Stopping in front of Mason, I leaned down to set my half-empty can between them, then backed away, all the while, keeping the knife hidden behind my thigh.

Once settled, I glanced up to see them still staring at me. Mason looked at the can then back at me. "Are you sure you're finished?"

Making eye contact with Kaden, I held his gaze even as I gave Mason a single nod.

Tension coiled between Kaden and me until I couldn't take it anymore and had to look away. I sucked in a deep breath. Had I been holding it the whole time?

"Oh, wow! She answered me," Mason said, his voice lacking mockery.

Mason grabbed a fork and took a bite of my leftovers then handed the can to Kaden. "So, if you're in a talking mood," he began, "do you want to tell us your name?"

Using my bag as a pillow, I laid down, pulling the blanket up over my chest.

"I'll take that as a no," Mason murmured.

I squeezed the handle of the knife hidden by my side and closed my eyes. I wasn't sure if I could sleep in the same room with two strangers. Two male strangers at that. But I had to get some rest. I had a long day ahead of me.

"Thank you." The sound of Kaden's deep voice surprised me, and I almost opened my eyes to look at him. Instead, I nodded again and turned away to face the wall. My body held stiff as I listened to the guys rummage around. The scraping of the can ended too quickly, then the rustling of bags could be heard as they cleaned up.

"I'll take the first shift," Kaden said softly, almost a whisper. "Probably best if you sleep over there."

There was a pause, then Mason grunted what sounded

like an agreement. "You're right. She'd freak if I got too close." The disappointment in his voice caused my muscles to tense.

"You go near her, I'll break your fingers," Kaden snapped.

My breath caught. Not only was his willingness to protect me surprising, he had also implied that Mason wasn't trustworthy.

"Of course I wouldn't," Mason cursed angrily. "I'm fucking ecstatic that she's here. Safe. I would *never* hurt her."

There was a long sigh. "I know. Just... I also know you get overly excited about things. And though you wouldn't purposely hurt her, if she were to wake up and see you laying too close, that would scare her. Scaring her, in my book, is the same as hurting her. So just keep your distance for now."

"I agree."

"Good."

My heart had raced the entirety of their conversation. This was the first time I'd heard so many words come out of Kaden's mouth at once. And the things he'd said? They made me feel.... safe. They made me want to stay. But I couldn't afford to feel that way. It was too dangerous. They hadn't tied me up, I was fed and had a roof over my head. Nonetheless, they'd essentially kidnapped me. They'd also saved my life. I might've been able to get away from that flesh eater on my own, but it had definitely been a close call. I owed them now.

At peace with the knowledge that neither of the men would bother me—tonight at least—I relaxed my shoulders and willed myself to sleep. In a few hours, I would make a break for it.

3

PINK AND ORANGE STREAKED THE SKY AS THE FIRST rays of morning sunlight brightened the sky. From behind, the darkness beckoned me to turn around. Instead, I hitched my bag higher up on my shoulder and moved forward. The guys weren't following me. I'd made sure of it. But a few seconds later, I couldn't help but double check. Nothing. My stomach twisted and I sighed, unsure if what I was feeling was disappointment or relief.

While Kaden had taken the first watch, just like he'd said, I'd rested. I couldn't call it sleep because it was so light my eyelids had fluttered open on and off all night. When Mason took his friend's place, I'd laid perfectly still and waited. Mason had paced for an hour or two, circled the house then went outside for a while. Eventually, he'd sat down in the room with Kaden and I. A few minutes later, his breathing had slowed. *Bad watchdog.*

Though he'd sounded asleep, I'd waited another half hour or so, listening to the men's soft snores. Then I'd carefully and silently got up. After a long glance at my quilt, I'd left it on the floor with an internal sigh and threw my bag over my shoulder. Repacking the blanket would've made too much noise.

Now I was climbing the fence that circled the local elementary school. Clearing the chain-link, I landed on my feet and glanced around. A bird squawked, and the light tinkle of a wind chime sounded in the distance. Not another living soul, or dead one for that matter, made their presence known, and I made my way quickly to one of the back entrances of the school.

Rummaging inside my bag, my fingers encountered the cool metal I was looking for. I pulled out a set of keys and unlocked the rusted deadbolt attached to the double doors, then jumped inside, shutting the door behind me.

My steps were silent as I swiftly made my way down the deserted hallway. Trash littered the floors and most of the classroom doors stood wide open. I kept a safe distance from the ones that were shut. I wasn't sure which rooms were worse. Behind the closed doors, the sound of shuffling feet sent a cold shiver down my spine. However, I did my best to keep my eyes from straying toward the rooms that stood open. At least the bodies had decomposed to mostly skin and bones by now.

I stiffened as I passed the one locked classroom that stood silent. It was the one with a broken window. The one I'd had to come through the first time. The memory of those children…

I shook my head and kept going, keeping my eyes forward as I listened for anything unusual. I spent most of my time here, but that was no reason to become complacent or lose focus. Bad memories could do that. It was best to just forget.

In the cafeteria, I found one of the utility closets and using the same set of keys as before, I unlocked the door.

Against one wall stood a large metal shelf with cardboard boxes containing my clothes. On the other, was a simple cot and a small nightstand. I emptied a shelf of its contents, pulling down the boxes before lifting the entire shelf off the wall and setting it down beside me. Hidden behind it was a cut in the drywall, making an uneven square. Digging my fingers into the drywall, I lifted the piece out, revealing a hole big enough to crawl inside. There wasn't room, however, because the fourteen by twenty space was filled with an assortment of food I'd stashed over the last six months. As far as food went, I was set for a long time. With a sigh, I opened my bag and filled it up with as much as I could carry.

Once the shelf was back in place, I sat on the cot. I had no clue why I'd come to the school to find shelter when there had been plenty of homes I could have lived in. At the time, it had seemed like a good idea. There had been no going back to my own house. It was haunted by bad memories now.

As I looked around the cramped closet, my chest tightened with loneliness for the first time in so long. I thought maybe I could stay, forget what I'd come here for in the first place, and hide. Again. Instead, I packed what clothes I could and the Dean Koontz paperback I'd left on the nightstand before locking the closet door behind me.

I grunted as I lifted the heavy pack onto both shoulders, but I also smiled to myself. My mission was only half-way complete and so far, it had been a success.

The way back out of the school was as easy as when I'd entered, but just as I pocketed the keys I heard the unmistakable sound of vehicles approaching. Flattening myself against the brick wall, I craned my neck around the corner.

Tires squealed as two large pick-up trucks swerved around the corner, stopping in front of the school. The first thing I noticed were the guns. They were pointed toward the sky, each held by dirty, rough looking men in the back of the cargo beds. Between the two vehicles, there were five of them all together. And more inside the cabs.

The men jumped out as the cab doors opened. As I counted them up, my heart raced. Nine. Nine heavily armed men. I swallowed hard, my fingers trembling as I dug them into the brick at my back. How the hell was I supposed to get past them?

The men stalked the front entrance, their guns pointing up as they scanned the area. When one swiveled his head in my direction, I jerked back, slamming the back of my skull against the hard wall. I winced but held perfectly still and quiet as I thought out a plan. The distance between me and the men wasn't all that much. Maybe fifteen yards. Could I outrun them?

I risked another peek. The men were facing the front of the school now. It looked like they were going to break in. Though my heart raced, I waited patiently. When they went inside I could make a run for it. I jerked my head back when one looked over his shoulder. The sound of glass shattering caused me to jump.

Once the last guy cleared the door, I took a deep breath, let it out, then ran. When I got close enough to the fence, I leaped, my fingers clamping painfully to the metal. I heard a shout behind me and my stomach dropped. I swung my leg over the fence and jumped. Behind me, the shouts were getting louder. They were coming after me.

Don't look. Don't look. Arms pumping at my sides, my breathing labored, causing my lungs to ache, but I couldn't stop. I made it to the road then cut through a patch of woods. Except, in order to get back to the house, I'd have to go out in the open again. Just as I sprinted across another two-lane road, an engine growled and a male, "Whooped," behind me. I glanced back, my eyes widening when I saw them gaining speed.

My feet pounded the pavement. They'd seen me, but the neighborhood was on the other side. It was the only way. I hefted the pack up on my shoulders, wondering not for the first time if I should ditch it. But then none of this would have been worth it.

Determined to get the food to Kaden and Mason, I hunched down and ignored the burning in my thighs as I pushed for more speed. I blocked out the sound of the men chasing me, my focus solely on the long uneven line of wooden privacy fences ahead. I leaped over a small ditch and sprinted into the field of dead grass, searching frantically for the spot I wanted.

Where is it? Where is it? I panicked. They all looked the same. Every fence. Every roof.

There!

The breeze flipped the slender gray cloth over to this side of the fence. At the last minute, I'd decided to leave the sock hanging on an exposed nail. I was patting myself on the back now. In my panicked state, it would probably have taken me longer to find the right house without it.

I sprinted forward, doing my best to ignore the growling engine in the distance and the hoots of excited men on a hunt. If I could just get to the house, we could hide, and they would give up.

Huffing and out of breath, I threw my bag over the fence, then leaped. The wood dug painfully into my fingers as I slipped. Gritting my teeth, I tightened my grip and used my toes to pull myself up. Ass backward, I slung my leg over the top then paused to look. The coast was clear. I couldn't even hear them anymore.

Sighing with relief, I quickly swung my other leg over the fence. But just as I was about to hop down, the world around me slowed. Cool fingers wrapped around my exposed ankle and pulled, causing me to gasp and instinctively yank back. Instead of getting away, I fell backward. My eyes widened, seeing only the wall of gray clouds above as I opened my mouth in a silent scream.

4

EXPECTING TO HIT THE GROUND, I FROZE WHEN INSTEAD my landing was softened midair. Then sanity returned and I began to fight. My elbow sunk into something hard and a grunt sent warm air blowing across my neck. Goosebumps spread across my skin, and I shivered. Flailing my arms, I pushed at the thing that held me.

"Hey! Stop! It's okay. It's me."

Every one of my muscles stiffened at the sound of the gruff voice in my ear. I turned to look at the man holding me in his arms. Mason stared down at me, his dark brows furrowed as he scanned my face. The lines around his mouth and eyes deepened. "Are you all right?"

My body slumped against him causing him to stumble back with the sudden weight. As he tightened his arms around me, I pressed my nose against his chest and breathed in deeply, letting his scent relax me.

"We thought you left us," he whispered. "We waited. Just in case. You left your blanket. I told Kaden you wouldn't have left your blanket if you hadn't planned on coming back. He didn't believe me, but he still wanted to wait. Where did you go?"

When I pushed at his shoulders, he let me get to my feet but kept his hands on my arms as I stumbled. Turning swiftly, I met his eyes, then pointed to the fence.

"What's wrong?" he asked.

I pointed again. However, when he only stared at me, I curved my fingers like a gun and pretended to shoot. Then I pointed at the fence again.

He shook his head slowly. "I don't know what you're trying to tell me. Just say it."

"Hey, what's going on?" Kaden came around from the side of the house, his steps faltering when he saw me. His expression didn't change, but his lips did press harder together causing them to thin.

"You came back," he said, sounding like I shouldn't have bothered.

"She keeps pointing at the fence."

Though Kaden's lack of enthusiasm for my return stung, I nodded along with Mason's words, pointing and pretending to shoot.

"See?" Mason said, his hands flying up.

"Yeah, I do," Kaden murmured, pushing past me to look over the fence. Just then, the growl of truck engines caused us all to glance up. When the guys looked at me, I nodded, eyes wide as I used my hands to tell them we should go inside. Instead, Kaden used his own hand gestures for us to duck down. Though we were on the other side of a six-foot-high fence, Kaden cleared that by at least two inches. Mason almost. And with the hilly terrain, we could easily be seen from the right angle.

Noticing my bag a few feet away, I reached for it, then

put my arms through the straps. When we ran—because we would have to run—we'd need the food.

Kaden peaked over the top of the fence, but for only a second before he was ducking back down.

"What is it?" Mason asked.

"Trouble," he replied tightly. Mason stepped up beside him and took a look, cursing under his breath.

Turning to Mason, his jaw tight and eyes stern, Kaden gestured toward the house. "Take her inside and hide. Do not leave her side."

Mason, his face more serious than I'd ever seen, gave Kaden a terse nod. Then he turned to me, jerking his head toward the house for me to follow. Gripping the straps of my bag, I swallowed hard then stopped to look back at Kaden.

Kaden's gaze locked with mine for a full five seconds before it flickered to my bag and narrowed. I let him have it when he held out his hand. His expression, flat and unreadable before, morphed into surprise as he pulled open the top flap. When he glanced back up, his lips were parted, his eyes wide, confused, but appreciative. Then it was all gone and his expression was even once again.

Hooking the flap back, he handed me the bag. "Go," was all he said.

At first, I just stared at him. "Come on," Mason said in a whispered shout just as the engines came too close for comfort, along with a few familiar shouts. "Go," Kaden growled. I went.

Inside the house, Mason pointed toward the stairs. "Come on. It's best to go up, I think."

Nodding, I followed him up and into one of the bedrooms. He shut the door behind us, then went to the window, pulling back the blinds to get a look. Not knowing what else to do, I stood in the middle of the room. It was pretty plain. Gray walls, a twin bed with white sheets and dark gray quilt with yellow flowers.

As voices grew louder outside, I shook my head and joined Mason at the window. I pulled back a blind and sucked in a sharp breath. Three men with guns walked below us. Their voices carried up, muffled, but clear enough to hear.

"I saw her go over this fence. We should check inside."

My heart skipped a beat, and I glanced at Mason. His face pinched as if he was thinking hard about something. Licking my lips, I looked back out the window. Where was Kaden?

Mason touched my shoulder and nodded at the closet. "See if you can hide in there," he whispered just as a shout outside caused us to still.

"Hey!" a man called out. "Is that her? Go. Follow her!"

Then silence settled over us, and the only sound left was our ragged breathing. When my shoulder brushed Mason's, my eyes fluttered up, catching his gaze already on mine. We stared at each other, just breathing, our arms now pressing against one another. My heart pounded, either from fear of the men looking for me or because of the man standing next to me, I didn't know.

Mason stiffened. "Shit," he exclaimed softly. That's when the smell registered. I followed his gaze to the smoke billowing under the door and gasped.

We both turned to the window at the same time, Mason reaching for the seal first. It slid open easily and we leaned over to get a look. There wasn't a soul that we could see, but the drop would be rough.

I looked over my shoulder. The smoke had thickened

and I could have sworn the heat singed the hairs on the back of my arms.

"We have to jump," Mason said unnecessarily. "I'll go first. That way I can catch you." I started to shake my head, but he began climbing out the window, ignoring my protest.

Once sitting on the window seal, feet dangling, he turned so he could face me, then let himself hang from his hands. Giving me small smile, he winked. "See you down there."

Pushing off the side of the house with his feet, he let go, landing on the grass with a roll before hopping back up. After looking both ways, he looked up at me and smiled triumphantly. Then he held out his arms and nodded. *Right. Time to go.*

After dropping my bag to the ground, I took a deep breath and slid out the window, sitting on the seal just like he'd done. Instead of turning around, I tucked my arms and jumped, trusting that Mason would catch me.

The drop was short. Nevertheless, it caused my breath to catch and my heart to race with adrenaline. Mason caught me easily, but when I expected him to set me back on my feet, he hesitated. He pierced me with the same smoldering look as before. Would he kiss me now? We shouldn't. For multiple reasons. The most imperative being how much danger we were in. But as his head dipped toward mine, I lost all sense of logic.

I gave a breathy sigh as his lips brushed mine. I'd barely gotten a taste of them when he suddenly tensed.

"Put down the girl and take a step back."

The command had my heart leaping into my throat, and I clung to Mason's shoulders as he placed me carefully on my feet.

"Come over here," the deep voice said.

I couldn't take my frightened gaze off Mason. Like a lifeline, our gazes connected, and I couldn't look away.

Lifting his hands up, palms out, he took a slow step away from me, then another, until he was too far for me to reach. The man who'd spoken grabbed Mason's shoulder and pressed a gun to his temple.

"There. That's better," the man said. His red beard was just beginning to gray, but the lack of lines around his eyes either meant he wasn't that old or he never smiled.

His dark blue eyes settled on mine. "Figured you were hiding in there. Didn't know you had company, though." He pressed the gun harder against Mason's temple, causing him to wince.

My back teeth ground together. For some reason this made him crack a smile. A small one.

"Don't like that do ya?"

Another man came up behind him, a shotgun held loftily over one shoulder. "Duke," he nodded to the guy holding Mason. "What do we have here?" he asked. His squinted eyes raked over me from head to toe. Then he licked his lips, grinning when my gaze narrowed. *Disgusting.* "Not much to look at, but you'll do."

The insult didn't bother me. I was more worried about my companion. Murder showed clearly in Mason's eyes. From the vein that pulsed wildly in his neck, he was seconds away from doing something stupid. I made eye contact and shook my head just enough for him to understand. *Don't.*

"The boyfriend's a problem," Duke said before speaking to me. "If you come to us without a fight, we won't kill him."

Movement in my peripheral vision had me glancing

that way. But only for a fraction of a second before I focused on the men in front of me again. Mason mouthed the word run. Seemed he was a mind reader, that one.

I turned on my heels and took off. As expected, I made it only a few steps before a hand clamped down on my arm painfully. As he yanked me back against him, I used the momentum to swing around with a raised fist. Pain exploded across my knuckles as I made contact with his nose. But ignoring the pain was easily done while hearing the satisfying sound of bones crunching under the hit.

His gripped loosened as he cried out, and I pulled out of his grasp easily enough while sending a knee into his groin. The hit caused him to make a choking sound in the back of his throat before falling to his knees.

"Feisty. I like that," Duke chuckled. "Beau, wipe the blood off your face and bring her over here."

Beau spit a wad of blood on the ground and sneered at me, a promise in his eyes. I wasn't about to find out what. Before he could stand, I bent down, simultaneously grabbing the knife in my boot as my other foot connected with his head. Then, with a flick of my wrist, I sent the knife flying toward Duke.

Wide and filled with confusion, the single eye stared back at me until the last light of life dimmed. Mason stepped sideways as Duke's body slumped to the ground at his feet. He looked between me and the dead roughneck.

Kaden, who had just stepped out of his hiding spot, said nothing. But his expression told me he was disappointed or disgusted, I wasn't sure which. It took a lot of strength not to clutch my chest and beg his forgiveness. Instead, I turned toward Duke's prone form. As much as I wanted to look away, I couldn't. I'd done this. I'd killed a man. Looking away would make light of what I'd had to do. Bending down, I gripped the knife's handle and slid it out, choking back vomit at the sight of the mess that was once Duke's eye.

Taking a deep breath, I stood on shaky legs and made my way back to the man lying on the grass, clutching his groin.

"I'll fucking kill you, bitch," he spat.

Squatting next to him, I lifted the knife. His eyes widened. "No," he whispered. But I had to. From Duke's own mouth, they admitted they didn't know about Mason and Kaden. If I let this guy live, he'd tell the rest of them. They were after me, and would no doubt give chase once they found their friends' bodies. But only me. Not the guys. I couldn't put them in danger. Not because of my mistake.

Mason said something, I wasn't sure what. A hollow sound had filled my ears as I carried out my deed. Then I wiped the knife on Beau's dirt stained shirt and rose to my feet. Chin high, I grabbed my bag and started walking.

It wasn't until about a mile outside of town before I finally stopped to empty the meager contents of my stomach onto the side of the road.

5
———

WE WALKED FOR DAYS, STOPPING ONLY WHEN exhaustion or hunger forced us. I didn't know where we were going, and for the first three days, I hadn't cared. Mason and Kaden were headed south, and I followed. I just kept walking, not seeing much of my surroundings. Not a care for when we'd stop. I wondered if this was how the flesh eaters felt. No purpose. Except to eat when hungry. Sleep when tired. Drink when thirsty. The only difference, I supposed, was that flesh eaters didn't sleep or drink. That I knew of.

I did remember a brief discussion between the guys. A couple hours after we'd fled the scene with the roughnecks, Mason had asked Kaden how many were left. He'd whispered the question as he glanced back at me. I'd pretended not to notice.

"Four," Kaden had replied, his voice just as hushed. "They were in the trucks so I hadn't been able to get to them. But I have a feeling they were part of a bigger group."

From that comment alone, I'd determined he'd killed

the other three. I'd ground my teeth together thinking of the anger in his eyes after I'd taken out Duke and Beau.

"Think they're after us?" Mason had asked.

"Yes. But they aren't looking for you and me." Kaden's gaze flickered in my direction.

Exactly, I'd wanted to shout. That was why I'd had to do what I'd done.

As the silence stretched between the guys, I'd begun to wonder... Had that been Kaden's way of saying he would hand me over?

The air had whooshed out of my lungs almost violently when he'd added, "If we stick by her, they might not notice who she is. None of them got a good look at her. And if we see them first, we can hide her."

For the first time in years, tears had prickled the corner of my eyes. I'd choked them back, of course, but I wouldn't forget it. I owed them. Again.

"Let's stop here for the night."

Glancing up at Kaden's announcement, I noticed we were coming up on an old, overgrown barn. Leaning to the left, it looked as if the trees were holding the structure up. The reddish-brown wood blended in with its surroundings. The roof was covered in red, brown, and yellow leaves. The same leaves that covered the ground. A gust of wind sent goosebumps over my skin. Yesterday, I'd had to pull out my jacket. I'd been so far inside my own head over the last few days, I hadn't paid close attention to the weather.

Kaden did his usual, which included searching the barn while Mason and I waited. When he returned, we were allowed inside. Then he spent an hour walking the perimeter, as he called it.

The inside of the barn was cool and damp but would

work for a night or two. With the dirt floor and the giant hole in the roof, it would be safe to make a fire too. It had rained earlier in the day, and the heavy clouds still cloaked the sky. If we waited until dark, no one would see the smoke or the flames.

Hungry, I searched for a makeshift table with no luck. Besides the remnants of hay littering the floor, the place was pretty sparse. Sitting on the ground, we began rummaging in our bags. We'd divvied out the food a day into our journey. The weight of the cans had slowed me down too much. Plus, if the three of us were ever separated, at least we'd have some supplies. The thought of running away again flitted across my mind. It was probably time. I should have left already.

I closed my eyes and blew out a calming breath. But when I opened them, I was unsettled in a completely different way. Mason's gaze held mine, searching deeply before falling to my lips. His eyes darkened seconds before he looked away.

I ignored the fluttering in my stomach and stared down at the food. Between us, we'd set three cans of soup and two bottles of water. I'd wanted to wait for Kaden, but maybe eating would keep my mind and hands off other… things.

Mason's voice caught me by surprise. "You had to do it," he said.

The meaning behind his words made my stomach flip. I looked away, my gaze landing on the open doorway. *Freedom.*

"You shouldn't have had to, though," he continued. "If I would have…" My eyes jumped to his as he trailed off. "The point is, I'm sorry. I promise I won't ever put you in that position again."

Not comprehending what he'd meant, my brows furrowed. Put me in that position? He didn't do anything. I was the one who had led those men right to us.

"You're safe with me," he whispered harshly. His eyes, full of guilt and determination, drilled into me as if I would refute his words.

My hands balled into two small fists. For the first time since I'd met him, I wished I could speak. I would tell him he didn't have to worry about me because I was leaving soon. A tiny voice inside my head said, *or maybe you would tell him not to worry because he already had your trust.*

"We okay?" he asked.

I didn't know what that meant exactly. What I did know was that he had no reason to feel badly about what had happened. To ease his mind, I nodded.

Bringing up my knees, I wrapped my arms around my legs, then rested my head on them as I looked at Mason. Eyes twinkling with mischief once again, he slid closer, until only inches separated us. I hid my grin against my legs when he pushed his shoulder into mine, causing me to sway. The grin turned to a full-blown smile when he did it a little harder. My hand shot out, catching myself before I toppled over. Bottom lip caught between my teeth, I sat up and pushed him back. He barely moved. But he did chuckle sweetly. His eyes, the color of autumn, I realized, squinted a bit and crinkled in the corners when he smiled. A smile that was damn contagious.

"Wimpy," he teased.

My shoulders rose and fell with silent laughter, and I shook my head.

"Hardly," a deep voice declared.

My smile instantly dropped as Kaden stepped inside the barn. He halted next to us, his gaze jumping between us before settling on me. When they narrowed, I scooted away from Mason.

I liked Mason. He was nice. Annoying, but sweet. Kaden, I wasn't sure about. He was as hot as Mason, that was for damn sure. And I could tell he was a nice guy. However, I got the distinct feeling he didn't like me. Not only could I feel his disapproval, but he'd yet to look at me without scowling. Another reason for me to leave them alone. It made no sense. If he didn't want me around, why had he forced me to come with them? And why did he do nice things for me? Like, lend me his blanket at night? Or offer me the first choice at dinner? The man was a conundrum.

"You have to admit, she was pretty bad ass," Mason replied. Then to me, he asked, "How did you learn to throw a knife like that?"

I shrugged and reached for my can of soup.

"It wasn't bad ass," Kaden argued. "It was stupid."

"Kaden," Mason warned.

"I had the situation under control," he stated to my bowed head. "If you had just waited, I could have taken care of them. What you did was dangerous and could have gotten us all killed."

The cold soup sliding down my throat turned to cement. I choked, then coughed.

"You okay?" Mason patted my back but I shrugged him off.

Not hungry anymore, I left the can in my spot when I stood, then made my way to a dry corner of the barn to make a place to settle down.

"That was shitty." Mason's harsh voice was hushed. "You need to apologize."

Kaden responded with one of his grunts.

Digging through my bag, I found an extra coat and a small pillow. My quilt had been destroyed in the house fire. My shoulders rounded, remembering. It was just a damn blanket, I told myself. Wiping my nose on my sleeve, I sat up straight.

It's the way things are now. Everything gets destroyed or taken away.

I caught Kaden watching me, and I looked away to slide on my coat.

"It's almost dark. Let's get the fire going," Mason sighed.

I would have helped, but Mason waved me away. When they were finished, he tried coaxing me to join them by the fire. I refused. The thought, *three's a crowd*, flitted through my mind.

While leaning against the wall, eyes closed, I pondered my escape. Was escape the right word? They hadn't held me captive. Not really. If I wasn't their captive, then how did I go about just leaving? Should I tell them, or just get up and walk out? Wait until they're asleep? I thought of Kaden's hurtful words. Definitely walk out, I decided. He deserved to watch my ass leave, knowing he was one of biggest reasons why.

Footsteps came closer before stopping next to me. Without opening my eyes, I took a deep breath through my nose. The smell of smoke mingled with an earthy scent I now associated with Kaden.

The air moved as he took a deep breath. "I'm sorry," he said softly, his voice coming from lower than I expected. I opened my eyes to see him crouching next to me, his blue gaze level with mine.

A deep v formed between his brows. "You did what

you had to do. You saved Mason and yourself. We owe you. Most people wouldn't have been able to go that far."

I tilted my head, not understanding. He'd said I'd almost got them killed.

My face must have given away my confusion because he nodded. "I only said what I did because I was angry. At myself. When I saw you and Mason being held by those men, it should have caused me to act. My instinct should have been to take those guys out. I wanted to. It killed me to see you two like that. But… I froze," he confessed.

He swallowed, his Adam's apple bobbing with the motions, then his voice lowered. "It was like seeing what happened to my family all over again." He hung his head, his breathing ragged as he was doing his best to hold himself together.

Surprised by how much he'd just opened up to me, I laid a shaky palm on the back of his head and stroked his hair as he took deep measured breaths. I wanted to ask him about his family. What had happened? Had he been there? But without a voice, I couldn't. And if I used sign language, he'd turn the questions around on me. Now wasn't the time.

Lifting his head, he gave me a sad smile that didn't reach his eyes. "I'm sorry," he said again.

I nodded my acceptance of his apology, then smiled when he held out a hand. I took it, and let him lead me to the fire to join Mason, who was leaning back against his pack, staring into the flames as if he hadn't heard the one-sided conversation between Kaden and me.

Using my pack, I laid sideways, facing the flames. The heat warmed my cheeks and caused my eyes to flutter shut.

"Are you hungry?" Mason asked me. "You didn't eat much earlier."

My gaze landed on Kaden. Of course, he'd been staring right back at me from across the fire.

"I warmed up a can for you," Mason continued.

When I nodded, he set it down in front of me with a spoon. I took a bite and would have moaned had it been possible. *Warm soup. Mmm.*

Mason chuckled. "From the look on your face, I'm assuming it tastes good?"

I nodded quickly and took another bite. Within minutes I'd finished the can.

"If you could have anything to eat, what would it be?" he asked.

I shrugged.

"Hmmm," he hummed. "I'd have pizza. An extra-large, loaded with pepperoni and sausage."

The three of us were silent as we thought about the heavenly pie he'd described.

"I'd have biscuits covered in sausage gravy, and a side of eggs and hash browns," Kaden said, playing along.

I pointed at him and nodded, my eyes rounding so he'd know I agreed with him. The corners of his eyes crinkled. Was he smiling? I couldn't tell from my spot. The flames hid half his face.

"That's what you'd have too?" Mason asked me.

Nodding, I laid my hands on my stomach and sighed. Biscuits and gravy were my favorite breakfast food. They were good for dinner too.

"Pancakes," Mason said.

"With real maple syrup," Kaden added.

Mason moaned. "Mmm, yeah. Dripping with melted butter."

My stomach growled causing the men to chuckle. I smiled and shook my head.

"Bacon," Mason continued. Was he ever going to stop? "And sweet tea. Damn, I'd love some tea."

With my belly half-full of soup and the fire keeping me toasty warm, exhaustion set in and I yawned. My eyes fluttered shut again. Mason continued to list all the foods and drinks he missed and hoped to have again, while I tried to ignore his words and let his voice become nothing but white noise. I nestled my back against my bag and began to drift off. But when he started naming his all-time favorite restaurants, I sighed.

A bark of laughter made me jump, and my eyes flew open in surprise. No longer on the other side of the fire, Kaden now stood next to my feet, and he was laughing. Shoulders jerking and eyes shining, he turned his smile in my direction. A beautiful smile that caused my breath to catch.

"What's so funny?" Mason asked.

"Now you know what I've been putting up with for months," Kaden said, his amused eyes still on me.

Not understanding his meaning, my brows furrowed and I began to shake my head.

"What are you talking about?" Mason's brows were furrowed as he looked back and forth between Kaden and me, but I didn't have an answer for him.

Smile softening, Kaden lifted his hands and signed the same sentence he'd spoken. *"Now you know what I've been putting up with for months."*

I sucked in a sharp breath. I jerked my gaze to his. He still smiled, his eyes reflecting amusement and something new. Something I wasn't sure I was ready to see.

I looked back down at his hands as he began signing again. *"You asked Mason if he ever shut up."*

Hand over my mouth, I glanced at Mason. He was still looking at us, his expression one of utter confusion

"Uh, is she deaf?" He turned to ask me, enunciating each word slowly. "Are. You. Deaf?"

I began to shake my head no, but Kaden beat me to the punch.

"No, not deaf. Mute."

I nodded, yes.

"Wow," Mason muttered. "That explains why you haven't made a single sound since we met you. Were you born mute? I have so many questions."

With a sigh, I nodded again.

"How about we let…" Kaden tilted his head. "What's your name?"

"Jane," I signed.

He graced me with another one of his smiles. I locked the image in my mind. I had a feeling those smiles were rare.

"Jane," he repeated for Mason's sake. "Let Jane get some rest. You can ask her your questions tomorrow."

The childlike pout on Mason's face would have made me grin, but a yawn took me by surprise. His pout disappeared. "You're right." He stood quickly. "Come on. Bedtime, Jane."

My arms flailed as I found myself being hauled up into his arms. Wide-eyed, I clutched at his shoulders so I wouldn't fall. At first, I was surprised, then indignant. Who gave him permission to touch me? I didn't need help walking. But as I registered the feeling of his arm beneath my thighs and the hand at my side, my anger melted away. He was warm and smelled like a man. Okay, he didn't smell fresh, but it wasn't all bad. He also smelled like camp fire and outdoors.

Fingers brushed the edge of my breast and I jerked. With the fire behind him, his face was now in shadow, but the desire in his heavy-lidded gaze was as clear as day. His arms tightened around me as I shivered.

"Here we are," he said, his voice turning to gravel.

I stood on shaky legs, refusing eye contact as I looked for my bag.

"Here." Bag in hand, Kaden stood next to Mason, his gaze dark as he looked down at me. That beautiful smile was long gone.

Taking the bag, I took a step back and gave them both a nod. Kaden turned on his heels and walked away without another word. My gaze stuck like glue to his back until he reached the other side of the barn where it was too dark for me to see him.

"I know I said this before, but I'm sorry about your blanket," Mason said, catching my attention. "You can have my sleeping bag if you'd like."

I waved away his offer. Again. Each night one of the guys would offer their sleeping bag, but I'd refuse, then wake up warm nevertheless, covered with a fleece blanket I hadn't gone to sleep with. No matter how many times I'd try to give that blasted blanket back, the guys would wait until I fell asleep to cover me again. It had become a little game of sorts. I shouldn't be so stubborn. But I couldn't help it. Every time I turned around I became more indebted to them. As soon as possible I needed to find supplies.

"Sure?" Mason asked. "We could share?" Though his voice teased, it also held a hint of hope.

I rolled my eyes and shook my head no.

"Can't blame a guy for asking." He shrugged. Gaze darkening once again, his smile slipped. "If you need anything, Jane, don't hesitate to ask."

Oh, damn. I could think of something I needed right now. I looked behind Mason to see Kaden sitting by the fire. Though his eyes were on the bright orange flames, I had the strangest feeling he was watching our exchange. And though I was seriously attracted to Mason, I couldn't help but feel guilty.

Looking back at the sexy man in front of me, I gave him a soft smile, hoping he'd catch the thanks, but no thanks. He nodded, his expression saying he got it. Then he went back to the fire with Kaden.

Laying down, I stared at the two men as they began to converse. They were both good men. Which was damn hard to come by these days. And they were sexy to boot. I didn't have a problem with sex. And Mason was interested. But... If we hooked up, I had no doubt Kaden would blow a gasket. Though I wasn't sure why. My mind screamed that maybe he was interested in me too. He had given me a few once overs. I rolled my eyes. *Yeah, right!*

Then my brain took me on a journey to a world I'd never imagined. A world where Mason and Kaden both wanted me. And I wanted them. And we acted on it.

I closed my eyes, letting my imagination take me on a wild ride as I fell into a deep sleep.

6

MY EYES FLUTTERED OPEN, WONDERING WHAT HAD woken me. In my corner of darkness, I let my eyes adjust to the muted blue moonlight that streamed through the hole in the center of the roof. The clouds must have cleared at some point. The guys had stomped out the fire, and the air held a slight chill. Not as cold as the day before.

With his back facing me, Mason lay on his side few feet away between me and the barn door, sound asleep. Sitting up, I looked down at the blanket that pooled in my lap and grinned. As I rubbed the soft fabric between my fingers, I raised my head to listen. My brows furrowed when the sound reached my ears. Singing. Someone was singing.

The dirt floor was cool beneath my bare feet as I tiptoed around Mason. The closer I got to the front of the barn, the clearer the voice became. Careful not to be seen, I leaned against the doorframe, my eyes focusing on the man bathed in moonlight. I shouldn't have been surprised at what I saw. Though I'd never heard him sing, I'd recognized his voice immediately. He sat on a fallen log next to the barn, his gaze on the woods in front of him. Absently, his hands moved, whittling a small piece of wood with a pocket knife. I gave the action a cursory glance before my attention went back to his face.

Deep and dark as the night, his voice rose and fell, gaining intensity as he neared the chorus. I recognized the lyrics as The Sound of Silence by Simon and Garfunkel. But the mournful way he sang it was like nothing I'd ever heard. Though he was holding back, each note barely more than a whisper, the passion behind each word that fell from his lips had me leaning heavily against the doorframe. I'd never heard anything so beautiful in all my life.

A mixture of sadness and longing creased his expression, luring me in. And the way his lips formed each word caused my longing to increase. My stomach clenched as an ache spread across my lower extremities.

I soaked in everything about the moment, until the last word was sung, a haunting refrain that lingered in the air and wrapped around my heart. As the night quieted, tears splashed to my cheeks one by one. And yet, as the silent tears stained my skin, my breathing had become shallow, and my nipples beaded beneath my warm flannel shirt. Eyes glued to his face, I sucked on my bottom lip and took slow measured breaths through my nose.

I must have made a noise because he slowly turned his head in my direction. I would have expected him to be surprised to find me watching him. But he didn't look it. His eyes, as haunted as the song he'd just sang, met mine and held. He didn't say anything. He didn't act as if to get up. He didn't move a single muscle. Didn't even blink. And yet… As if he'd shouted my name and demanded me to come to him, I found myself moving in his direction.

Maybe it had been the full moon, or maybe it had been the song, but the air was heavy with desire, drawing us together like magnets. His fingers were cool against my heated skin as they skimmed my shoulders, taking my shirt with them. His lips followed, the touch whisper light. My belly trembled when he reached for the snap of my jeans. And when I stood naked before him, I didn't feel the chill in the air or the icy breeze that claimed the autumn night. Only the heat of his stare, my desire, and my frustration as it increased with each heartbeat.

Hot, wet heat enveloped my nipple sending me rocking back on my heels. Kaden gripped my hips pulling me back before sliding one palm over my backside as he worked on the opening of his pants. I basked in his touch, in the way he kissed and suckled at my breasts. Then I was astride him, the steel length of him pressing at my weeping center.

Not able to wait another second, I grasped him in my hand, giving him one long stroke before placing him at my entrance. He moaned, long and low as I took him inside me with slow deliberate movements. Inch by glorious inch, he filled me perfectly, causing my eyes to roll back in pleasure.

Our eyes met, and my grip on his shoulders tightened, the feel of fabric beneath my fingers unsatisfactory. I yanked at his shirt, pulling it up and over his head so that my naked breasts pressed against his flesh. The intensity in his gaze was too unnerving, so I lifted up, wanting to bring us only pleasure. I didn't want to think about tomorrow, or the regret I would undoubtedly feel. I didn't want to think about anything. Nothing but pleasure.

His fingers dug into my ass, and my lips parted on a gasp as he forced me back down on his cock. My pelvis titled, grinding against him until my clit found the friction it craved. The fabric of his pants rubbing against my thighs only heightened my sensitivity.

I lifted up, and he pulled me back down. Over and over again we played the game. Until the tension pulled tight, ready to break. But it held strong, and I gritted my teeth, moving my hips faster.

Grasping my neck, Kaden pulled my head down until I faced him instead of the moon. His thumb pulled at my chin, then his mouth was on mine. Hot and hungry, he devoured me with his kiss and the tension snapped.

As my mouth opened in a silent scream, Kaden's lips and tongue trailed down my throat. A shudder ran down my spine causing my inner muscles to spasm a second time. Stiffening, Kaden grunted, then lifted me off his cock before burying his face in my neck. It had been irresponsible of us to not use protection. If he even had any. But for a moment, a tiny moment when his release warmed the front of my stomach, I'd wished he could have come inside me. Now that would have been stupid.

Exhausted and overwhelmed by the intense encounter with Kaden, I leaned my head against his shoulder. His arms were wrapped around me, holding me tightly. Safety. Not a feeling I was used to.

"Jane," he whispered against my neck. I held him tighter so he wouldn't say anything else. It had been the first word spoken that night, and if I had any say in it, it would be the only one.

A shadow passed the dark entrance to the barn, catching my eye. Feeling me stiffen, Kaden's palm ran up and down my back as if to soothe me. But as much as I enjoyed his touch, nothing could ease the guilt twisting my stomach into knots. What had I done?

7

"MORNING, SUNSHINE!"

Wiping the sleep from my eyes, I sat up to look at the man with the too cheerful voice. The bright sunlight streaming through the roof of the barn caused me to wince. Damn it! I'd overslept.

"*What time is it?*" I signed, forgetting Mason didn't know what I was asking. The dimming of his smile had me rushing to find another way to ask. I tapped the top of my wrist. The hand gesture must have made perfect sense because his grin spread.

"We let you sleep in. It's almost lunch time. Hungry?" he asked.

Nodding, I eyed him suspiciously as I took the bag of jerky from him. I wasn't imagining things the night before. He'd seen Kaden and me.

Maybe he's not as into you as you thought, Jane. That was entirely possible, I agreed with myself.

As I chewed my breakfast, I watched him carefully. He grabbed a bottle of water and took a sip before passing it to me. His gaze landed on my mouth as I drank. Seeing the blatant hunger in his stare caused me to swallow hard sending the water sliding down the wrong way. Coughing, I set down the bottle and wiped at my mouth.

"Are you okay?" Mason patted my back firmly until the coughing stopped. "Hate when that happens," he said.

Pointing at my pack, I waited for him to look back at me before using two fingers in a walking motion, hoping he knew what I was asking.

His head tilted to one side. "You want to know when we're getting on the road?"

Smiling, I nodded.

"We will in a little while." Leaning toward me on his knees, he said, "You have a beautiful smile." When my cheeks warmed, he chuckled and sat back. "Will you show me how to say that in sign language?"

My face was flaming, but I lifted my hands and showed him. He tried a few times before he finally got it right.

"That's amazing. Will you show me more, later?"

As I nodded, I reached up to scratch my scalp, frowning when I encountered the greasy feeling between my fingers. Hopefully, we'd find somewhere we could bathe soon.

"What's wrong?" Mason asked.

Shaking my head, I showed him a chunk of my dirty hair.

His lips formed an O of understanding. "Dirty?"

"A bath would be nice," I signed.

"She said a bath would be nice," Kaden repeated from across the room.

As our eyes met, I blushed. More than just my hair needed a good cleaning after last night. The corner of his mouth tilted up in a knowing smile and I had to look away. I already felt guilty about the night before. No way would I flirt with Kaden. Especially in front of Mason. Although, he wasn't acting at all like he cared.

"Thanks, but I don't need you to interpret," Mason snapped before turning back to me with an easy smile. "A bath, huh?" he asked, his voice back to being soft. "I think we all need one."

The difference between the way he'd spoken to Kaden and then to me was so significant I couldn't help but glance at Kaden. He looked as shocked as I did. Or maybe a bit more surprised than me. As far as I knew, he didn't know Mason had seen us together.

"The river isn't far from here," Mason continued. "I saw a spot less than a mile back that had calm enough waters to use for bathing. The water will be pretty freaking cold, but it's a warm day."

It was warm, I realized. *"Okay,"* I signed.

Mason smiled, then rose to his feet. "Great! Let's go. I'll take you."

"I'll go with you," Kaden broke in.

Mason stiffened, his eyes narrowing a fraction as he turned to his friend. They stared at one another for several seconds before Mason finally gave a clipped, "Fine."

Was it fine? I looked between the two men and had a feeling that things were far from fine.

———

"If we continue south then turn west when we hit—

"No. We should keep moving southwest in a diagonal path. It will save us time."

"Exactly the opposite, actually. Your route gets us

farther into the mountains sooner than we need. That'll slow us down."

"I disagree."

Gritting my teeth, I hitched my pack higher on my shoulders and sped up my steps, hoping to get far enough ahead of the guys that I wouldn't be able to hear them anymore. Their bickering hadn't let up since we'd left the barn, and I'd just about had enough.

"Hey, Jane! Wait up!"

Ignoring Mason's request, I pushed through some underbrush toward the sound of rushing water. When I reached the bank, I stood still and breathed in the refreshing scent. A small smile lifted my lips. In this one spot, in this one moment, with the birds chirping and the hush of running water as background music, the world was once again a beautiful place.

First Mason, then Kaden, came to stand next to me. "Wow," Mason murmured. "This place is gorgeous. Don't you think… Jane?" He called when he noticed my retreating back.

I waved away his question as I walked down the bank toward the stream pool. I wasn't trying to be rude, and I wasn't mad at Mason, but listening to the two of them arguing all morning had taken its toll. Quiet. I needed quiet.

Dropping my bag to the ground, I surveyed the area, then pointed to a large cluster of rocks. The men must have understood, because they both nodded, then headed that way. The rocks were large, tall enough to be our natural shower curtain. Undressing, however, couldn't be done in private.

Turning my back on the guys who stood only a few feet away, I quickly stepped out of my clothes and laid them over my backpack. A breeze caused my skin to prickle, but it wasn't so bad. It felt more like spring than fall. I was more worried about the water. Mountain rivers were notorious for their icy waters. Which was why I hadn't jumped in yet.

I dipped the tip of my toe where the water lapped gently on the bank, then pulled it back quickly as I sucked in a sharp breath.

"What's wrong, Jane?" Mason yelled. "The water too cold for you?"

I'd totally forgotten they were behind me. Both watched me, unabashed at being caught in the act. Kaden lifted an eyebrow, while Mason's grin stretched ear-to-ear.

Pursing my lips, I rushed headlong into the freezing cold water. Laughter following me, as my eyes widened in shock. Mason bent over, holding his stomach. Even Kaden chuckled.

"Cold?" Mason called.

I gave him my best glare, which only made him laugh harder. I wasn't really mad. It was pretty ridiculous the way I'd jumped in the water just to hide something both had probably seen a million times over. And them laughing at me was ten times better than the constant bickering.

Every thought in my head came to a frozen halt when I realized I'd missed something very important. While they'd been watching me undress, they hadn't been idle. Both were halfway to naked themselves. I had to blink to confirm what I was seeing was real. Not only was it real, I was seeing double. Double the broad shoulders and thick biceps. And abs. A lot of abs were on display. What was it about the V line that could make a girl forget her own name? Yeah, I was seeing double all right. Double the trouble.

Though shivering, my insides were warming right up as I shamelessly stared. Hey, why not? They'd had their show, now it was my turn. Unfortunately, as they began sliding down their pants, both had glanced up and caught me in the act. After getting a wink from Kaden and an eyebrow wiggle from Mason, they turned around, showing off their perfect round asses instead. A pretty damn good consolation prize, in my opinion.

Kaden looked over his shoulder and gave me a grin I'd never seen from him before. It was the type of grin a man gave a woman he'd known intimately and wanted to again. Flushed, I turned away, but not before I caught Mason's glower.

I sighed. These wicked thoughts were so unlike me. The longer I stayed with the guys, the stranger I felt. It was like I didn't even know myself anymore. But denial wasn't pretty. I'd slept with Kaden, but I lusted after both men. What did I do about that? Truth was, I probably *shouldn't* do anything. I sighed again.

A splash from the other side of the rocks was followed by a shout. "Holy shit!" Mason exclaimed.

I smiled as the men made the plunge into the cold water.

"Fuuuuuuu…" was Kaden's response.

My shoulders shook as I silently laughed at their antics. Then I leaned back and ran my fingers through my hair, letting the river wash away the dirt and grime. My body had gotten used to the cold water and I no longer felt the shock of it. Instead, it felt invigorating. Though that might have something to do with the way my body had heated up at the private show the guys had given me.

"We should get on the road soon," Kaden said, catching my attention.

Mason snorted in response. "I'm surprised you're ready to move on so quickly."

"What do you mean? The sooner we get to your Uncle's place, the better."

"I won't be going with you," Mason said softly.

"What?"

Dread sat heavy in my stomach, and I moved to the edge of the rocks to get a better listen.

"You and Jane should go without me," Mason continued.

"What is this about?" Kaden asked.

"I just think three's a crowd, is all."

I sucked in a startled breath. Then my shoulders slumped against the side of the rock as the silence stretched on the other side. How did I fix what I'd done? Mason and Kaden couldn't split up. Whenever I thought of the two men, they were always together. Best friends, through thick and thin.

I closed my eyes and hung my head in shame. I couldn't get in between them. I had to leave. It was the only way.

"So you know," Kaden whispered.

"Yeah," was Mason's murmured reply.

"Mace…" The thickness in Kaden's voice caused my eyes to well with tears.

"Was it just a one-time thing?" Mason asked, hope lifting his voice.

Part of me wanted Kaden to say yes, it was nothing but a one night stand. That we'd been out of our heads. The full moon had made us do it. Or better yet, that I'd seduced him.

Another part of me, a deeper part, was scared to death that he would admit just that. That I meant nothing more than a silent screw under the stars.

I wiped at my nose, holding back the sniff that might remind them I stood mere feet away and could hear every word.

"Truthfully, Mace," Kaden said. "I don't know."

I blew out the breath I'd held. He answered exactly how I would if I was being honest.

"That tells me it was more than just one night," Mason said. "And I can't watch the two of you together. I thought I could, but... I just can't."

I'd had enough. I couldn't let Mason leave. His place was with Kaden. I was just a tag-a-long that had over stayed her welcome.

Kaden and Mason faced each other, but their gazes were on the water below. As I got closer, the splashing water alerting them to my presence. Their heads jerked up, their eyes widening at my presence.

"I'm mute, not deaf!" I signed.

Upset, I put my hands on my hips and glared at the men. Neither noticed. I followed their stares, looking down at my chest. My dark, rose colored nipples jutted out, rock hard from the icy water. Goosebumps covered the milky flesh surrounding them and I shivered as a cool breeze blew over my flesh.

Looking back up, I pursed my lips and brought my hands in front of my breasts to sign, *"I think I should leave."*

Both men blinked as if coming out of a trance. Mason blushed and looked away. Kaden, however, showed no signs of embarrassment. Instead, he nodded. "Good idea."

It hurt at first, him agreeing so quickly that I should

leave. What had I expected? I'd ruined his friendship with Mason.

Taking a deep breath, I ignored how both men glanced at my heaving chest and signed, *"Thank you for everything. I won't forget it. Or you. Either of you."*

Turning quickly before I lost the nerve, I began wading back to shore.

"Wait! Jane!" Kaden called behind me. "I thought you meant you were ready for *all of us* to leave."

"What did she say?" Mason asked.

"She's leaving."

"Leaving? Without us?"

"Leaving *us*," Kaden corrected.

The break in his voice gave me pause, but I couldn't do this to them. I couldn't split them up. *What if it didn't have to be that way?* I shook my head at the image of both of them naked and hovering over me. No, I couldn't ask that of them. What if they thought I was depraved for wanting two men at once?

"Jane, talk to me. What's going on in that head of yours?" Kaden said, coming up behind me.

Pausing at the edge of the shore, I stared at the tiny pebbles below my feet, my mind swirling with fantasies and realities. Shivering, I wrapped my arms around myself. I wanted what was best for Kaden and Mason. I liked them too much to ruin their friendship. But I was a selfish woman as well. Could I ask them? I wasn't ignorant. I knew they both wanted me. Was it enough?

"Jane," Kaden whispered. I turned to find him standing right next to me, his face contorted in pain. "Why are you leaving?"

"I messed up," I signed. *"You and Mason are fighting because of what we did. I'm sorry."*

"What did she say?" Mason came to stand next to his friend, his expression just as worried.

Kaden sighed. He knew I was right. I looked back and forth between the men, my nerves getting the better of me. Maybe it was best to just leave before I did any more damage.

"She's leaving because of what happened last night. Between us," Kaden explained.

Mason sucked in a breath and looked away. His hands landed on his hips as he turned away from both of us. When he finally faced me again, I mouthed, *"I'm sorry."*

"No," he whispered as he squeezed his eyes shut and shook his head. "No, I'm sorry. You did nothing wrong. It's why I should go—"

I cut him off with a shake of my head. *"No,"* I mouthed.

His pained expression deepened. "Please, Jane. I can't stay and…" he trailed off with a sigh. "I'm sorry. But it's for the best."

My jaw tight, I glared at the annoying man as my hands flew into motion.

"She said it doesn't matter if you leave or not, she's going. So, you might as well stay with me," Kaden repeated what I signed.

"Don't do this, Jane," Mason groaned. "It's safer if you pair up."

Mason was more stubborn than I'd thought. My only option was to make them my offer. I rolled my eyes internally. *You're such a martyr, Jane. You know it's not your only option. You want this. Don't pretend like you don't.*

Taking a deep breath, I let it out slowly. *"It's safer in pairs. But three is better,"* I signed.

Kaden's gaze moved from my hands to my eyes.

Something in my stare must have alerted him to my meaning because the corner of his mouth lifted, and his gaze darkened.

Without looking away from me, he said, "Three *is* better." The wicked gleam in his eye said he meant the innuendo.

"Jane," Mason sighed, oblivious. "I know I said that once, but it just won't work. Things have changed between us—"

Before he could finish the sentence, I stepped forward and pressed my lips to his.

8

————

MOUTHS FUSED TOGETHER, WE STUMBLED INTO THE barn, our bags and clothing falling to the ground with a thud. Mason shoved my wet jeans down my legs, his lips never leaving mine. Until my legs tangled up, and with a gasp, we both tumbled to the floor. Mason twisted, taking the brunt of the fall and my weight. As I hit his chest, I winced, then smiled at the wide-eyed look he sported. A sudden grin split his lips, then he was laughing.

The arms banded around me tightened as he pulled me up for a kiss. I sipped at his lips, enjoying the taste of him, my hips rocking against the solid length pressing against my stomach. My nipples scrapped against the soft hairs on his chest, and I wiggled harder, trying to get as close as possible.

Mason groaned into my mouth. "Jane," he whispered.

I deepened the kiss, causing him to groan, but eventually, he was able to pull away.

"Wait, wait,' he murmured breathlessly. "We need to slow down."

I shook my head no and leaned in for another kiss

except he pulled away. I blinked, more curious than hurt. I tilted my head and mouthed the word, "*Why?*"

Sighing, his head hit the floor with a thump. As he stared up at the broken roof, his Adam's apple bobbed when he swallowed. I licked my lips, wanting nothing more than to taste him there too. But he had something he needed to get off his chest first. I understood. And I didn't want him to be uncomfortable. It was already a strange situation. So, I waited, somewhat patiently as he ran a hand over the top of his head. His fingers slid easily through the wet strands of hair...

"Uh, Jane," he croaked, "could you hold still for a minute?"

Realizing I'd been slowly rubbing myself against him again, my face flamed. *"What's wrong?"* I signed.

Mason's brows furrowed as he stared at my hands.

"She wants to know if you've changed your mind," Kaden said above us, sleeping bag in hand. He laid it flat next to us, then grinned as he pulled off the wet jeans still clinging to my ankles.

Mason rolled us onto the puffy fabric, placing one arm around my waist to keep me pressed to the front of him. "No, of course not," he replied, pressing a kiss to my cheek.

"Good," Kaden nodded. "I'll give you some privacy."

Tilting my head, I asked, *"Where are you going?"*

Kaden knelt beside me. Pulling wet strands of hair off my cheek, he gave me a soft smile. "I'd love nothing more than to stay with you right now," he said, correctly reading the true meaning behind my question.

I smiled shyly, looking at him through lower lids. I would have liked nothing more than for him to stay too.

"But I think you and Mason need this time to

yourselves. And I'm not comfortable with the idea of no one keeping watch."

"Oh," I mouthed.

"Oh," he repeated with a smirk.

Leaning forward, he pressed his warm lips to my forehead. I closed my eyes and tilted my chin, accepting the second kiss on my lips. He pulled back before it could get too heated. Unfortunately.

Kaden chuckled as he stood, the sound deep, and dark —that of a man who knew he'd gotten under a woman's skin. "Pouting doesn't suit you, Jane." His eyes darkened. "Then again... Mason, do something about that pout, would you? Before I do."

"Yes, sir," Mason grinned.

My eyes connected with Mason's for only a second, long enough to see how much he wanted me before his lips descended. I clung to his naked shoulders, pulling him closers as he sucked my bottom lip into his mouth.

"I wanted us to go slow," he breathed before nipping at the same lip. "To make sure you want this as much as I do." Pulling back, he looked down at me, his heavy-lidded gaze jumping from my swollen lips to my eyes and back again. "Tell me you want this, Jane. Tell me you want me."

Cupping his cheek, I kissed him softly. Then I grabbed his hand and placed it over my mound, pressing until his fingers slipped through my wet folds.

"Fuck," he whispered. "You're soaked."

Biting my lip, I nodded and moved my hips against his hand. There was no question about how much I wanted him.

Groaning, Mason hovered over me, pressing my legs

apart so he could fit his hips between them. I shivered as the cold wet fabric of his pants brushed against me.

"Shit." Rolling off me, he jumped up and stripped off his cargo pants.

Spread out naked on the sleeping bag, I laid still, waiting, shivering at the loss of his warmth. I watched him with blatant hunger in my eyes. And as he couldn't seem to tear his gaze off of mine, I was pretty damn sure he noticed.

He dropped to his knees at my feet, leaning over to mess with something in his bag. I would have paid attention but I was too busy staring at the thick cock that stood so hard and straight, it pressed against his stomach.

"There we go."

I tore my eyes away from the object of my desire to see Mason looking at me with a dazed expression and holding up a small square packet. When I licked my lips, he sucked in a stuttering breath.

My movements were slow and deliberate as I sat up and leaned toward him. I kept eye contact, wanting him to see what was coming. I felt like a predator. I *was* a predator. And Mason, my prey. His throat moved as he swallowed hard. Yeah, he'd figured it out.

I knelt in front of him and dipped my head to nibble on his collarbone. A guttural groan rose from his throat as I licked my way down his chest. The packet he held fell the floor as he reached for my hips. His grip tightened, his nails digging into my skin. I liked the slight pain. Loved it, actually.

Skimming my hands up his arms and over his shoulders, I let him kiss my neck for a moment before flipping him to his back and straddling his waist. His eyes widened, but the way they flashed darkly told me he'd enjoyed my little show of power.

A moan parted his lips when I ground against his pelvis, my own lips parting at how good it felt. I could easily slide him inside of me. But first, I had other plans.

The sudden halt in my movements made Mason's eyes clear as he blinked up at me. I couldn't have that. I wanted him mindless with pleasure. Leaning over, I placed open-mouthed kisses over his chest, then nipped at his nipple. He hissed, and I laved away the sting with my tongue before sliding down his body.

The grip on my hips loosened, but he kept contact with my skin, letting his fingers drag up my sides as I moved farther down. Once I was face to face with his cock, though, his hands dropped to his sides. As I stared, his cock pulsed and a bead of pre-cum formed at the tip before running down the side. I licked my lips eliciting a loud groan from the man below me.

"God, Ja—" Mason groaned the rest of my name as my tongue ran up the side of his cock, licking away the trail of cum. Closing my eyes, I groaned internally. He tasted like nirvana.

Not able to wait another second before tasting him again, I closed my mouth over the tip, sucking lightly before slowly lowering my head until he reached the back of my throat.

Mason's gasps and groans were like music to my ears and I rewarded them by swallowing. As my throat tightened around his cock, he called out my name and threaded his fingers into my hair. He gripped the strands until my scalp stung. It felt amazing.

I knew part of his excitement had nothing to do with my skills. He'd probably gone a long time without sex.

Still, I found joy in being the one to give him so much pleasure.

I sucked in a breath through my nose then slid back up, teasing him with my tongue. The move must have been too much for him because he pulled me up, growling as he rolled on top of me.

"That wasn't very nice," he said, his eyes sparkling in the dim light. I lifted an eyebrow. "Okay, it was very, very nice," he amended. "But it also felt like torture."

Reaching down, his fingers parted my folds. My hips bucked into his hand as he hit the perfect spot.

"Mmm," he murmured. "Feels like you tortured yourself as well."

I nodded repeatedly, then threw my head back as a sudden orgasm ripped through me.

"Perfect," Mason whispered into my neck before leaning away. I would have pulled him back if I hadn't heard the unmistakable sound of a wrapper being opened.

Seconds later, he was back. After lining up his latex covered cock with my dripping entrance, he braced himself with his arms above me. I spread my legs wide and tilted my hips, but he held perfectly still until I made eye contact. The intensity in his gaze blew me away. Long gone was the laid back, fun loving Mason. The Mason above me with his cock poised to take me at any second looked dangerous.

"I want you to see exactly who's about to fuck you, Jane."

My lips parted as I sucked in a quick breath, the ache in my core intensifying. His words were dirty and a little degrading, and I would have kicked his ass had he said them outside of this moment. But hearing it spoken when he was actually about to fuck me? I loved it. And I let him know by tilting my hips, pushing the head of his cock in just a hair more.

Mason gave a little growl, then plunged the rest of the way inside me. The stretch and burn of him filling me so fast felt amazing. As amazing as it had been the night before with Kaden. I'd thought for sure one or the other would be better. That I'd figure out I had no real connection with one of them. However, this moment with Mason shattered that theory. How was I ever going to get enough of either of them?

Deep and measured, Mason's thrusts kept me on the verge of orgasm. His lips found each of my rosy nipples. And when he chose one, he sucked on the tight peak, increasing the suction each time he pushed inside me. I arched so far up, I felt cool air move over the damp skin of my lower back, before the tension became too much and I broke.

Clawing at Mason's back, I came once again. If the first orgasm had been a stick of dynamite, then this one was made of ten times the amount. It was painful and glorious and lasted forever.

When the room came back into focus, Mason was still on top of me, his head buried between my neck and shoulder. Our breaths were fast and shallow and our skin felt slick with sweat. Overall, I gave the sex an A+.

Lifting his head, Mason's eyes twinkled down at me. "I hope you did something because I couldn't hold out any longer."

My shoulders shook with my silent laughter and I gave him a playful shove. How could he have missed the world exploding around us?

"Hey, between your silence and my own earth

shattering orgasm, I wasn't a hundred percent sure," he said, grinning down at me.

Lifting my chin, I asked for a kiss and wasn't denied. His lips were warm and soft and his tongue had moves that made me wonder where else he could utilize them. Mason groaned into my mouth and his cock began to harden once more inside me.

Just as I was ready to roll Mason over to start round two, a shadow fell over us. We ripped our lips apart to see a scowling Kaden staring down at us.

"Playtime's over," he said. "We've got company."

9
———

The goofy smile on Mason's face vanished as the first sounds of clicking teeth reached our ears. Fingers still on the button of my jeans, I stilled, my eyes flying to Mason as the noise grew not only in pitch but in numbers. How many were out there?

"I could use a little help out here!" From outside the barn, Kaden gave a shout, then growled as he, no doubt, fought for his life.

Adrenaline shot through my veins, spurring me into action. I finished dressing as quickly as possible, then went to my bag for weapons. Not having time to strap on an ankle holster, I stuffed a dagger into my boot, then pulled out a bundle of fabric wrapped in an old sweatshirt. Once unwrapped, I dropped the shirt and gripped the handle of the machete, testing the weight as I gave it a shallow swing. Then I quickly repacked my bag, sans machete, and threw it over my shoulders.

When I turned around, Mason was nowhere in sight. Assuming he'd already joined Kaden, I followed the escalating sounds of battle to the barn entrance and stopped cold. I'd never seen so many flesh eaters at once. Twenty or so staggered out of woods, while even more came from a field to the north.

Before I could find the guys, one stumbled toward me, its yellowed teeth snapping. I could have described it, but I'd learned long ago not to think of them in those terms. They weren't people any longer. It didn't matter if their pretty flowered dress was now ripped and covered in blood, or how lustrous their long brown hair used to be. They were dead now.

So, when my blade sliced through her skull, I couldn't think of her life before. If I did, I'd end up just like her.

A masculine shout had me spinning around. The men were trying to hold the flesh eaters back. The numbers were staggering and continued to grow. I rushed to help, swinging my blade into the mass of bodies, taking down a few, but as one went down, another would take its place.

"Where did they all come from?" Mason shouted over the deafening clicking noise.

"I've no fucking clue," Kaden grunted as he stabbed one in the temple. I turned to decapitate one of my own. "When I came to get you, there were four… five at most coming out of the woods. Then this."

"Shit!" Mason yelled.

I turned in his direction and was almost knocked to the ground when bony fingers grabbed my shoulders. Teeth snapped inches from my nose, and I jerked my head back as I shoved the machete into its stomach and pushed it off of me. A quick blow to the head and it was down for good.

"Jane!" Kaden called for me. I finished off another and rushed toward him just in time to kill the one coming up from behind.

Kaden looked over his shoulder and gave me a nod. He started backing up, and I followed, keeping the flesh eaters in front of us.

"See that hill behind us?" he asked.

Glancing back, I nodded. It was bigger than a hill in my opinion. More like a mountain with that incline.

"Head up there. The trees will keep you covered well enough. Stay hidden until we catch up."

When I stopped walking, his lips pinched with disapproval. I didn't care. He couldn't force me to abandon them. Just as I was about to tell him so, his eyes widened seconds before he shoved me behind him. He took care of the flesh eater easily enough, and when he turned around, he looked furious.

"You could have been killed!" he yelled as we began walking backward again.

"I'm not leaving you," I signed. *"I can help."*

"I know you can. But there's no way we can kill them all. There's too many. If you go now, they won't follow. They'll be too busy with Mason and me." When I narrowed my eyes, he sighed. "We'll be right behind you. I swear."

At that moment, Mason called out and Kaden took off to help his friend. I followed, but when I got there, Kaden had taken care of the three that had surrounded Mason. Mason, though covered in sweat and blood, looked okay. When he saw me, his face twisted. "Get out of here, Jane!"

I hesitated once again, long enough to take out a flesh eater who came too close. We had to get out of here, but did I dare leave without them? Splitting up didn't sound like the smartest move in my opinion.

The mob of walking corpses seemed to grow as they

pressed us backward. As my blade sliced easily through another skull, a distant rumble caught my attention. It was hard to tell with all the clacking of teeth surrounding us, but it sounded like…

"Shit!" Mason yelled. "It's them!"

My head snapped in the direction he was looking, my eyes widening in fear. The flesh eaters had pushed us up an incline and I could see over their heads and past the barn. Rolling across the field, taking out flesh eaters in its wake was an all too familiar pick-up truck.

"Go!" Kaden said to me. "We'll catch up."

More flesh eaters rounded the other side of the barn and the guys cursed.

Waving me toward the mountain at my back, Mason yelled, "Go! We're coming."

It wasn't until they began running in my direction that I finally did what they had asked.

As the ground began to incline, I dug deep to keep up the momentum, but eventually, I had to slow. It was becoming more of a climb than a hike at that point, and I had to reach for a thick root to pull myself up. I'd gotten halfway before I allowed myself to look back. The trees had thickened so much I couldn't see the flesh eaters anymore. The sound of their teeth hadn't disappeared although the roar of the truck's engine had. What worried me, however, was the absence of my two men.

Leaning against a tree, I took a moment to rewrap my machete and slide it back into my bag, before continuing my climb. By the time I reached the top of the incline, my leg muscles were screaming and my fingers ached.

One more, Jane. One more. Stretching to reach, I dug my fingers one last time and pulled with all the strength I had left. My toes pressed into the dirt and rock to help propel me up and over the crest.

Once on flat ground, I rolled onto my back panting. My lungs were on fire and my muscles burned, but I'd made it. Now I just had to find Kaden and Mason. They'd been right behind me. Or so I'd thought.

"I wasn't sure you were going to make it for a minute there."

My eyes snapped open at the voice to see an unfamiliar man smiling down at me.

"Hi," he said, "We've been looking for you."

10

OLDER THAN ME, MAYBE IN HIS LATE THIRTIES OR EARLY forties, the skin around his eyes and lips wrinkled deeply when he smiled. His short beard was scattered with gray, but his dark, chin-length hair hadn't been affected by age yet. And his hands. They were calloused from years of working with them, I assumed.

The feel of his rough fingers against the skin of my arm as he hauled me to my feet, sent my stomach rolling. Swallowing hard, I ignored my need to vomit and searched for a way out of this. It was happening so fast. I was still trying to catch my breath from the climb. My lungs worked overtime as I sucked in air, and black spots danced before my eyes, warning me that I needed to calm down.

I gasped when he tore my bag from my back and pushed me against the nearest tree. It hadn't hurt, but the way he stepped close, crowding me, sucked all the oxygen out of my lungs.

Like a deer caught in headlights, I stared wide-eyed up

at my captor. He placed his hands on either side of my head, caging me in.

"I don't know what they were talking about," he murmured almost to himself as he leaned closer. "You're a pretty little thing. I thought so when I first saw you at the school." My whole body trembled when he rubbed his grizzly cheek against mine. "Maybe if I'm nice, you'll come with me willingly."

One of his hands lowered to brush against the side of my breast. "Mmm," he hummed in my ear as he gripped my waist and pulled our hips flush together. I closed my eyes, unwilling to think about what pressed against my stomach. My heart raced, and tears prickled my eyes, but I'd finally caught my breath and caged my fear long enough to allow my anger to take over.

He made a happy sound in his throat when I gripped his shoulders, thinking I was complying. *Wrong, asshole!* I brought my knee up sharply into his groin, smiling when he let out a croaking sound. When he slumped to the side to grab himself, I slipped past and made a run for it.

Fingers grasped the upper part of my arm and threw me against the nearest tree, and I realized too late that I should have reached for the knife in my boot instead of running. This time, he wasn't gentle. The breath whooshed out of my lungs as his body crashed into mine. His legs kicked mine apart and he pushed his hips against mine, effectively keeping me from kneeing him again. He gripped my wrists and slammed them against the tree above my head. My mouth opened in a soundless cry as the bark bit into my skin.

The harsh lines around his eyes deepened as he scowled down at me. "That was a mistake," he bit out. "I was trying to be nice. Now we'll have to do it the hard way."

Though he wasn't as big as Mason or Kaden, he did outweigh me by at least seventy pounds. There was no way I could get away from him. All I could do was wait for him to make a mistake. Maybe if he let go of my wrists I could jab him in the eyes. His hands tightened painfully as if he'd read my thoughts. Then he transferred my wrists to one hand so the other could slide down my body. Gritting my teeth, I turned away from his triumphant glare as he palmed my breast. Tears leaked from eyes when his squeezed too hard.

"Why so quiet?" he asked. He slid his hand under my shirt and pushed up my bra. He pinched a nipple between his fingers, giving it a harsh twist. My lips parted, but of course, my cry was silent.

"Why aren't you screaming?" he snapped. When he continued inflicting pain on my breast without receiving the sounds he expected, he reached for the button of my jeans. "I know how to make you scream, bitch!"

Through my tears, I could barely make out his expression. His voice held no compassion. I didn't doubt for a second that I would suffer in the worst ways by this man's hands. For the first time in my life, I wished for someone to save me. I couldn't do it myself this time. I pitched my body forward, yanking as hard as I could, but he used his weight to pin me down. As more tears spilled down my cheeks, I begged silently for Kaden and Mason. Where were they?

I was brought back into the moment by the sudden jerk in the man's body. His grip on my wrists loosened and I pulled away just as he slumped to the ground. His hazel eyes, wide and glazed over, stared straight ahead. Dead. He was dead.

My gaze fell on the arrow sticking out of the back of his skull and I backed up, putting the tree I'd just been held against between me and whoever had shot that arrow. My neck craned as I looked around the tree, searching for what could be either my savior or worst nightmare. If they'd had the skill to take down my attacker, they wouldn't be easy to get away from if they wanted to hurt me too.

Seeing and hearing nothing out of the ordinary, except the occasional bird or squirrel, I pressed my forehead against the tree. What did I do now? I couldn't call out to them. If I ran, they might shoot another arrow. I glanced down at my dead attacker. No matter the why, I was grateful for whoever had saved me.

"Jane!"

The sound of Mason's voice had me spinning around and waving for them to get down. They were coming from the same direction as the arrow, and my heart leaped in both pleasure at seeing them and fear that they might be the archer's next victim.

The men saw me right away and began jogging, their smiles bright. They weren't smiling for long. Kaden noticed the dead guy first. Before he could ask, I grabbed them both and pulled them with me behind the tree. It didn't come even close to offering us all protection, but I couldn't bear to see them out in the open.

"What is going on?" Mason asked.

"Archer," I signed to Kaden. I pointed to the arrow sticking out of my attacker's head. Both Kaden and Mason looked from him to me, their gaze narrowing on

the state of my clothes. "Looks like he got what he deserved," Mason clipped.

"Are you okay?" Kaden asked.

Since the moment they'd called my name, all I'd wanted to do was fall apart in their arms. But that wasn't me. Instead, I used the bottom of my shirt to wipe my face and gave him a stiff nod.

His eyes on mine, Kaden reached under my shirt to put my bra back in place. Though his movements were gentle, the cloth scraped over my battered nipple, causing me to hiss. He paused, his teeth grinding together as he did his best to finish without hurting me more. When he reached for the button of my jeans, I pushed his hands away and turned around to do the job myself.

"He's one of the roughnecks we've been running from," Mason said. "Did you see who shot the arrow?" I shook my head no. "Well, whoever it was is gone now." He looked up at the darkening sky. "We should get out of here too."

Nightfall approached and the adrenaline from my attack had faded, leaving me hurting everywhere. After the long hike and climb up this damn mountain, I needed to lay down. But I needed my bag more. It still sat on the ground where my attacker had thrown it. I hobbled past the dead man, surprised at the short distance I'd run from him. I was ashamed of how little I'd fought. I wasn't a weakling. I knew how to fight off an attacker and how to run and hide. I'd done it before. How had this time been different? How could I have allowed *this* man to get the best of me?

When I turned, Kaden was right behind me, with Mason not too far away. They were watching my back, their eyes on our surroundings. Protecting me. I frowned.

Had I become dependent on them? Were they the reason I hadn't fought harder? Because I'd been waiting on my rescuers?

Kaden turned his head just in time to notice my expression, his eyes widening in alarm. I could only imagine what he saw. Rage, shame, guilt... pain. Kaden, usually so put together himself, looked startled. Upset even. So, when he reached for me, I schooled my features to mask those feelings and walked past him.

For the first time in years, I was vulnerable. I couldn't allow them to do that to me. Not now. In this world, being vulnerable got you killed.

11

———

WE HIT A STRETCH OF ROAD LEADING US TO SEVERAL small cabins. They were vacation rentals, all with contrived names carved into their signs. *Bear's Den, Bear's Creek, A Bear Affair...* Someone had a thing for the furry beasts it seemed.

"Be right back," Kaden said before jogging toward one of the cabins. I pointed my flashlight at the sign, my brows lifting at the irony. *Three Bears Getaway*. Nice.

"How are you holding up?"

Hearing Mason behind me caused me to sigh. I'd been avoiding him, both of them. Between the attack and the realization that I might be depending too much on the guys, I'd had a lot to think about. I still wasn't sure where my head was at. But Mason didn't deserve the silent treatment. Neither of them did.

I turned to let him know I was okay and instead my jaw became unhinged. The beam of my flashlight hit him square in the face and he winced, but I couldn't move. He looked awful. His face was pale and a tad green and sweat had beaded across his forehead. The dark circles under his eyes spoke of days without sleep, yet I knew that wasn't the case.

He coughed, the move causing him to stumbled to the side. Rushing forward, I held him steady. The heat coming off his body had me touching his forehead. He was burning up!

Mason grabbed my hand and placed a kiss on my palm before tucking it under his arm. "I'm okay," he whispered. His voice held none of his usual confidence.

Hearing Kaden return, I began helping Mason toward the cabin. Kaden rushed forward to help, his expression not what I expected. Had he known Mason was sick this whole time? Mason stumbled and we paused until he could get his bearings. It might have been pitch black for most of the hike here, but how had I not seen this? He was a wreck!

Once inside, Kaden and I led him to the nearest bed. "No," he grunted as we helped him lay down. "Jane gets the bed."

I shook my head, but other than that, Kaden and I both ignored him. Leaving Kaden to help Mason get more comfortable, I searched for candles and got lucky. I pulled my bag off my shoulders and dug for a pack of matches. Successful, I lifted the glass off the hurricane lamp and lit the wick. The now illuminated room revealed the man's shadow next to mine. I wasn't surprised. I'd heard him walk up.

Kaden's hands hovered over my shoulders. When I didn't pull away, he laid them down gently and leaned in to kiss my neck. Tilting my head, I gave in to the touch, only briefly.

His hands fell from my shoulders as I turned to face him. "*What's wrong with Mason?*" I signed.

As he stared at me, I noticed the lines above his brow had deepened. Worry lines. My gaze scanned his face. Those lines weren't the only ones to stand out. Had he aged so much in only a day?

"What's wrong?" I demanded.

Instead of answering, he pulled me against his chest. His arms wrapped like steel bands around me, squeezing so tightly I gasped for breath. He eased his grip but continued to cling to me, his cheek resting on top of my head. This was so unlike the Kaden I knew, that I began to panic.

Unable to make sense of what was happening, I clung right back. However, it wasn't long before I was holding on for a different reason. My shoulders slumped, my muscles losing the fight to keep standing. Then the floor swayed beneath my feet. Kaden caught me, lifting me up and into his arms with ease.

"I knew you were about done for," he said softly against my head. "You need to rest."

Though as tired as I was, I still wanted to know what was happening with Mason. *"Is he sick?"* I feebly signed, my eyelids flickering as I did my best to keep them open.

Kaden gently lowered me to the bed and kissed my forehead. I turned my head toward Mason. The bed was huge, a king size. I hated that he was so far away, and I was too tired to move. He gave me a weak smile but otherwise said nothing. His silence was enough to cause my heart to race.

"Shhh," Kaden pressed on my shoulders until I lay back down. "He just needs some rest." He and Mason exchanged a look I couldn't decipher before he looked back at me. "Both of you do."

Pulling a blanket over my legs, he picked up one of my

hands. His jaw clenched as he stared at purple bruises beginning to bloom on my wrists. "If he weren't already dead, I'd kill him," he stated. Then, with an infinite tenderness I'd not seen from him before, he placed a healing kiss on both wrists before standing.

"Get some sleep," he whispered. "I'll take first watch."

———

It was the moans that woke me up.

I opened my eyes to a darkened room. As I looked around for a window to determine how close to dawn we were, I instead caught sight of Mason. Still lying on the other side of the bed, his body had curled into a fetal position facing away from me. He made a sound, a deep guttural moan. The same moan that must have woken me. A sob caught in my throat. This wasn't just a head cold.

Just as I was about to roll over to check his temperature, a hand caught my wrist and I jerked back. Kaden stood next to the bed looking down at me. It was too dark to see his expression, however, the anxiety rolled off of him in waves.

"I was just about to wake you," he said quietly.

Pulling my wrist from his gentle grasp, I signed, *"He's worse."*

"Yes," was all he replied with.

Blowing out a breath, I asked, *"Why? What's wrong with him?"*

"Let's talk out here," he signed back.

With a hand on my arm, he helped me from the bed. But before leaving the room, I looked back at Mason. The sun was just rising, affording me enough light to see the extreme pallor of his skin. I sucked in a breath through my teeth. If it weren't for his rapid breathing, I would have thought he were dead.

Kaden shut the door behind me, then pressed at the small of my back to move farther away from the room. Once in the kitchen, I turned on him. *"Tell me what's going on,"* I demanded.

The thing I was still trying to figure out about Kaden was how he could hold so much inside of him. His expressions, actions, even his words rarely gave me a sense of what he was really feeling. So, when his face crumpled, tears springing from his eyes as if the dam holding it in had finally burst, it scared the shit out of me.

When he turned his head away, as if ashamed, I leaped forward to offer comfort. With my arms wrapped around him, I couldn't sign. Instead, I pleaded with my eyes for him to tell me what was going on.

He sniffed back the tears and pulled me closer, pressing my head against his chest. I sighed, listening to the thump, thump, thump of his heart. I hadn't realized how much I needed this. How I'd needed him as much as he'd needed me. But the luxury of being in his arms was short lived.

When he finally answered my question, I was thankful he still held me in place. Because if he hadn't, I wasn't sure if I would have fallen to the floor sobbing or kicked his ass.

"Mason was bitten."

12

———

I SHOULD HAVE KNOWN. WE'D FOUGHT A HORDE OF flesh eaters and hours later he was deathly ill? Didn't take a Ph.D. to figure it out. But I'd selfishly been thinking about no one other than myself and hadn't seen what was right in front of me.

Kaden had pulled back the blankets and shown me the bite. It was red and swollen. Infected. And the location couldn't have been worse. Upper chest. Meant whatever those things infected us with would hit the heart and enter the blood stream quicker.

I gripped Mason's hand, trying to offer him reassurance. Though the gesture was probably more comforting to me than it was to him. Or maybe I was really tethering myself to him so I wouldn't do what I'd always done when things had gotten hard... run.

My gaze moved over his face, taking in the sheen of sweat and the circles under his eyes that continued to get darker. He hadn't woken since I'd come in. And he wasn't moaning anymore either.

Next to me, Kaden shifted in his chair. "He begged me

to keep quiet about it and let you sleep with him last night. I kept watch. I'm surprised it's taking this long." His sentences weren't put together well, but who could blame him? His friend was... He was going to... Mason would be...

"Shhh," Kaden hushed me as he wiped at the tears streaming down my cheeks. "Don't think about it."

I wanted to roll my eyes. Don't think about it? What else was there to think about?

"Hey," Mason croaked from the bed, causing both me and Kaden to jump. "I'm not dead yet."

"That's enough out of you," Kaden said playfully, a suspicious catch in his voice. "We're having a moment here."

Surprised, I looked at Kaden. His wink accompanied a sad smile. I understood. Keep things light. For Mason's sake.

"You hittin' on my girl?" Mason breathed, his eyelids cracking open enough to peek out.

Kaden shrugged. "Can you blame me?"

Mason's gaze landed on mine. "No. Can't blame you at all."

Picking up on the game, I signed, *"No fighting, boys. There's enough of me to go around."*

The guffaw Kaden let loose caused Mason to crack a smile. "What did she say? Damn. I hate that I couldn't take more lessons." His limp hands moved on his stomach as he attempted to sign the only thing I'd taught him. *"You have a beautiful smile."*

My smile had already wilted. But for him, I tried again.

"Thank you," he whispered. "Now what did she say?" he asked Kaden.

"She told us to stop fighting. We could share," he paraphrased.

Mason's chuckle turned into a series of coughs that had both me and Kaden up and hovering, unsure what to do.

"I'm okay," Mason croaked, coughing once more before lying back with a sigh. Just as we were about to relax back into our seats, we stiffened once more at a sound from outside. A car door.

Kaden rushed to the window and drew back the curtain. With a curse, he stepped away and turned to Mason and me, his expression one of resignation.

"Is it them?" I asked, my heart racing. How did they keep finding us?

"I think so," he said, then shook his head. "I don't know. If it is, we're fucked."

A groan from the bed had me rushing to help Mason as he struggled to sit up. I had to hold back a gasp when I put my arm around his shoulders. The heat from his body was so extreme I didn't know how the man was still lucid.

"Lay back down," Kaden hissed.

"We have to leave," Mason said. He started to swing a leg off the bed. Or tried to. He stopped when his breathing became too labored.

"There's no way we can get out of here in time," Kaden said carefully, but Mason was no dummy. The implications of that statement hit home. Mason would have to stay behind. That wasn't acceptable.

Kaden was strong. He'd have no problem hoisting Mason over his shoulder. Except, how fast could he run carrying more than two hundred pounds? If we each took an arm, we could help him together. I stared at Mason still trying to catch his breath from sitting up in the bed. There was no way he'd make it. He'd pass out before we got out the door. And again, how fast could we move?

"They're only a few cabins down from us," Kaden said from the window as if he were reading my thoughts.

Not fast enough, I answered myself.

"You two need to leave," Mason said from the bed. "Leave me. I'm dying anyway."

I shook my head no at the same time Kaden growled, "No. I'm not leaving you."

"You have to," Mason croaked, then turned his gaze to me, as if to follow up with, *"She needs you"*. Or maybe I was projecting. I shook my head no for not only Mason's benefit but for my own as well. I didn't need Kaden. Or Mason for that matter. However, I did want them. Major difference. I sighed, knowing it was more than that. I may not have needed them; however, I did care about them.

Knowing what I needed to do, I waved to get Kaden's attention. *"Did they see you fighting the flesh eaters yesterday?"* I signed.

"I'm not sure."

"They'll kill you," I signed.

"They won't hurt us." Kaden's gaze held mine as he said the exact thing I was thinking. "If you're not here, we'll be safe."

The words were like a punch to the gut, but so true I couldn't refute them. The only way they had a chance to be safe was if I left.

Mind made up, I nodded and went for my bag.

"No," Mason croaked. "Kaden. She can't go alone."

Kaden ignored his friend's protest and snatched his own bag from the floor. Throwing it on the bed next to Mason, he began rummaging inside, his movements fast and efficient. He pulled out the wrinkled map I'd seen him and Mason look at a dozen times. My gaze jumped from the folded paper he was pushing in my direction to his pleading stare.

Taking my hand, he pressed the map into my palm until my fist closed around the paper automatically. "This is a map of where we were headed. Go there. It should be safe. Or as safe as any place is, I guess." Then he turned around to zip up his bag.

"Take it," Kaden said when I hesitated. "I've memorized the way." Then he gripped my shoulders and looked me dead in the eyes. "If it is safe, you stay there. I will do everything I can to follow. I promise." I held his gaze a little longer, memorizing the way the tiny flecks of gold burst amidst the blue. He looked away first. "I'm sorry," he whispered. "I can't leave Mason."

Placing my hand on his arm, I gave him a sad but understanding smile, then signed, *"I would never ask you to."*

Then I turned to look at Mason. His face was a little rounder than Kaden's, with higher cheekbones. It made him look perpetually happy. Even when sick. He watched us, his deep brown eyes more clear than I'd seen since we'd gotten to the rental cabin. "Go, Jane. We'll be right behind you," he croaked.

No one in the room believed the lie, but we all pretended it was true.

We'd been standing frozen in the moment, fear and sorrow thickening the air, but the voices outside were becoming louder. Time had run out.

"Hurry," Kaden said to me, panic now setting in.

Backpack securely on my shoulders, I shoved the map into my pocket, then turned to him. My gaze flew over his face, taking in the sharp lines of his jaw, and the way his top lip pressed in more than the bottom when he was stressed. Like he was now.

"Bye, Jane," he signed. Not *see you soon,* or *I'll be right behind you* like they'd said before. No, this was goodbye for good. We all knew it.

Not knowing what to say, I turned away from him and rushed to Mason's side. After kissing his lips, I pulled away quickly to press another lingering kiss to his forehead, telling him without words that I'd never forget him. Then I stood, and without a backward glance, I ran.

13

I DIDN'T RUN FAR.

"It's for the best."

The words were Kaden's as I'd crawled out the bedroom window. I could only assume they were for Mason, but that hadn't stopped the phrase from playing on repeat in my head ever since.

"It's for the best."

It *was* for the best. I couldn't disagree.

"It's for the best."

Didn't mean I didn't hate him just a little for saying it out loud, though.

I slid to the ground and rested my head against the side of the cabin. I should have run. As soon as my feet had hit the ground, I should've taken off. Luckily, this side of the cabin butted up against an outcropping of trees and large boulders. Probably kept during construction to add a sense of privacy for vacationers. Whatever their reasoning for keeping it, it would be an advantage during my getaway. Especially with nothing but a steep drop on the back side of the building. However, I wasn't ready to leave. Not yet. I had to know if Mason and Kaden were safe.

As voices drifted from beyond the cracked window above me, I listened carefully, ready and willing to fight if necessary. Unbeknownst to me, my presence wasn't needed at all.

Kaden had gone out the front entrance, and at some point, had let the unfamiliar men inside the cabin. Not having heard the first part of the conversation, I was surprised when he'd brought them in to meet Mason. My shoulders tensed, worried they would kill him on sight. Yes, he was already dying, but Kaden would fight them and I doubted he'd win. I wasn't sure yet how many there were. Still, the odds weren't in his favor.

"As I told you," Kaden said, "he's very sick. We're in no shape to fight."

"And as I told you," a deep, accented voice replied, "we are not here to cause trouble." After a moment of silence, he asked, "Bitten?" The man's tone held a surprising amount of sorrow for someone he'd never met.

"Yes."

"If you need one of us to—"

"That won't be necessary," Kaden interrupted with a touch of anger.

"Fair enough. We won't bother you much longer. Like I said, we only wanted to introduce ourselves to put your minds at ease. We were searching for supplies. Not trouble."

"That's good to hear," Kaden replied.

There was a moment of silence before a throat cleared. "Is there anyone else in your group?" The same man asked.

Kaden's voice didn't waver. "Nope. Just us."

"Then I would offer you sanctuary. We have a couple of doctors that can look at your friend. Make him comfortable, at least."

My brows lifted at the proposition.

"Naahir, right?" Kaden asked, his voice skeptical. "What's the catch?"

"None," Naahir answered. "It is a safe place. But to be honest, we need more people willing to search for supplies and defend our home. People like you."

I snorted to myself. Right. Nowhere was safe. Who was this guy? And how could he think someone like Kaden would believe something so—

"We would be grateful."

The reply was so quick, without a shred of hesitation, it caused the air in my lungs to still. I tuned out the rest of their discussion, my gaze fixated on the trees as I wrapped my arms around my middle and brought my knees up slowly.

Kaden's easy acceptance of the man's offer shouldn't have hurt so much. They deserved to be helped, to find sanctuary. The logical part of my brain understood that Kaden had to be careful. I still wasn't sure if those were the same men who'd been searching for me. And he would assume I was long gone by now. But the selfish part of me wondered how Kaden could move on so easily. Would he even look for me now?

I shook my head. Selfish, selfish thoughts. Mason was dying and all I could think about was my stupid heart.

Standing, I blew out a breath and pushed all the emotional bullshit away for another day. The good news was those men were not going to hurt Mason or Kaden. Instead, they were offering the men I cared for a safe place to stay.

I couldn't bring myself to look in the window. However, I did give the small cabin a last glance before I left.

"It's for the best."

The anger I wanted to feel at the two men who'd dragged me out of my hiding spot, claiming we'd be safer together, and who had eventually left me alone miles away from home, just wouldn't ignite. Maybe I would see Kaden again, maybe I wouldn't. And Mason... I turned away from the cabin and the men inside who'd changed my life. I couldn't think about Mason now. First, I had to survive. And to survive, I needed to leave.

It was for the best.

14

As the car coughed and sputtered to a final halt, I sat back against the worn leather seat with a sigh. As much as I'd wanted to turn tail and run home after I'd left the guys, I'd been smart enough to see the danger in that move. Besides, what had I really left behind? It might have been my hometown, but it hadn't felt like home in a long time. So, with nowhere else to go, finding this supposedly perfect place he and Mason talked about had been a good an idea as any. Though, I'd had serious doubts Kaden would follow through on his promise to follow me.

Once I'd made the decision to start heading west, finding a working vehicle became the first priority. A bit of a challenge in the middle of nowhere. The few cars I'd run across were either out of gas or wouldn't start. I hadn't realized when I'd left my two travel companions how close we had actually been. According to their map, we could have been in Yellow Creek within two hours. *If* we'd had a car. Luckily, I'd found this rust bucket. I patted the cracked steering wheel. Though it puttered out too soon, ten to fifteen miles on foot was better than eighty.

Though the wind felt like ice outside, the sun shone brightly, warming the inside of the car to sauna levels. I wasted no time getting out and saw the flesh eater immediately. It took a second for it to notice me. Once it did, it changed directions.

Leaning back into the car, I grabbed my machete before securing my bag on my shoulders. Then I ate up the space between me and the flesh eater, taking it down in one swing. The silence afterward was a relief.

There were no more walking corpses, however, there were two cars pulled off the road up ahead. However, after an hour of trying, neither were drivable. I did find an unopened bottle of water, so there was that.

I kept the machete in hand—I'd learned my lesson last time—and began walking. If I continued following the road I was on, I'd end up in a Robbinsville. I'd never been there, and I didn't think it was a very large town. Just in case, though, I decided to skirt the edges. The larger the city the more flesh eaters or people I'd have to deal with.

I saw the high school in the distance and shuddered at the memory of my last school experience. I could have used more supplies, but I couldn't bring myself to check there. Eventually, I did run across a convenience store. Not much was left, but I was able to find a couple more bottles of water and a few snacks. I also found duct tape and nylon rope. I grabbed both as well as the matches and the few lighters that were left up by the registers.

I made one last round to make sure I hadn't missed anything, ignoring the clicking teeth and thumping of hands that came from behind the walk-in refrigerator. As soon as I'd entered the store, I'd noticed them. They were trapped, though, and didn't pose a threat. However, if I'd taken care of them, I might have heard the sounds coming from outside sooner.

Once done with my search, I was ready to get going. There were a few cars out in the parking lot I wanted to try cranking up. Maybe I'd get lucky.

As I moved to the exit door, something big and covered in fur jumped up, slamming into the glass. I fell backward on my ass, sliding on the linoleum a couple of feet before I realized what it had been.

The German Shephard's paws pressed against the door, his nails leaving white scratches on the glass as he barked and growled at me from the other side of the door. The flesh eaters in the walk-in went nuts. Their hands banged against the glass doors faster and harder, their teeth chattering grotesquely.

Standing on shaky legs, I picked up the machete I'd accidentally dropped when I fell, then I slapped the glass, hoping the dog would back away. Instead, he snarled, licking his lips as slobber dripped from his jowls. Then his barking became more erratic as he pushed against the door over and over again, his teeth clattering against the glass. I took one step backward then another. I wasn't leaving through that door.

Just as I was about to turn around to find the back exit, I was thrown onto the floor face down. Pain exploded across my cheek as it slammed against the hard linoleum, and I swear my vision receded. Still, I fought the flesh eater as it snapped his jaws at the back of my head. My elbow connected with its shoulder, pushing it half off of me. Enough that I was able to flip onto my back, but I wasn't able to get completely out from under it. The flesh eaters were nothing but rotten corpses that couldn't move faster than a crawl, yet somehow they were supernaturally strong.

I wrapped my hand around its throat, using all of my strength to keep its snapping teeth from finding flesh. In my peripheral vision, I saw the machete that I'd dropped again and reached for the knife, but my fingers only brushed against the handle. I wasn't close enough. And during all of this, the noise inside the small convenient store became deafening. The flesh eaters in the walk-in refrigerator were so loud now they drowned out the barking dog.

The thing on top of me snapped again, and this time a chunk of my hair got caught in his teeth. I reared back, my head slamming into the hard floor. Stupid, stupid move. Spots danced before my eyes and my limbs tingled with the first signs that I might pass out.

I heard the muffled sound of a crash just before glass rained down on top of me. My first thought was that whatever it was meant I was in trouble. But between one frightened heartbeat and the next, the flesh eater on top of me was ripped away.

As soon as its weight lifted, I scooted back, my eyes widening. It had been the dog that had broken through the glass, and he was making a snack out of the flesh eater. Gagging a little, I turned away just as the walk-in's doors cracked then shattered, letting loose a group of ten or more walking corpses into the main part of the store.

Scrambling to my feet, I wobbled as I tried to gain my balance. I was dizzy, and my vision wasn't so clear, but there was no time to wait. The store was small. Extremely small. And those flesh eaters were only a couple of body lengths away.

I snatched up the machete and staggered towards the

door. Gripping the edge, I climbed through the hole the dog had made, wincing as shards of glass dug into my palm. I ignored the pain to look back at my savior. The German Shephard had finished with the flesh eater but I didn't look to see what or how much was left. Instead, I sent him a silent thank you as he let out a growl and leaped at the group that was converging on me.

I collapsed through the door with a grunt, my palms scraping the rough pavement as I staggered to my feet. The dog yelped behind me. Just as I expected, there were too many of them. I had a bad feeling he wasn't going to make it.

The first flesh eater to fall through the door met my machete head first. I pushed his body to the side just as another followed. Realizing this was the perfect way to get rid of them and help my new furry hero, I stood to the side, knife ready as they came through the door. Then the clicking sound behind me registered and I turned in horror to see a horde of flesh eaters coming our way.

A soft whoosh of air next to my ear had me spinning around. The feather end of the arrow stuck straight out of the forehead of the flesh eater that had been right behind me. On the other side of the parking lot, the archer readied her next shot, pointing it directly at me. I ducked just as the arrow whizzed over my head and struck the next walking corpse.

I couldn't help staring. The girl looked smaller than me, and couldn't have been more than sixteen, yet she yielded that bow and arrow as if she'd been trained her whole life. She would have looked bad ass with her black leather jacket and ripped jeans if she weren't back dropped by a pale blue minivan.

This was the one who'd saved me? Twice? My eyes

narrowed. There were a lot of miles between here and our last encounter.

"Come on!" The girl shouted in a voice deeper than I'd expected. "I don't have enough arrows to get 'em all."

She slid opened the back door of the van, then gave a sharp whistle. "Poco, come!" The German Shephard leaped through the door, his brown coat soaked through with blood. Though as he trotted to his owner without so much as a limp, meant he was unharmed.

So, the dog belonged to the archer. Somehow, that alone eased some of my concerns, though I wasn't sure why.

Squinting, the girl put a hand to her forehead to block the sun. "Are you coming or are you planning to become dinner?"

A quick glance told me the horde was fast approaching. I took out the last flesh eater stumbling through the door behind me, then turned to follow the girl. The chances that she'd saved my life just to kill me were slim to none. Or so I hoped.

15

————

Once we'd gotten far enough away, the girl insisted we stop to take care of my injury. I hadn't even felt the cuts in my hand until she mentioned them, then they stung like a bitch. Thankfully, the cut hadn't been too deep, just a bleeder.

While she poured bottled water over the wound I listened as she prattled on about how much trouble I was. As if she were my keeper. Though my response should have been anger, I couldn't help but smirk. She reminded me of Mason.

The girl dug through her bag until she found what she was looking for with an "Ah ha!" Then she ripped a strip of fabric from a worn t-shirt and wrapped it around my hand.

"That should do it," she said.

Parked on the shoulder, we sat on the ground next to the van. The dog laid down a few feet from us, stretched out on the ground beneath a ray of sunlight. As he let loose one of those big sighs dogs do that either means they're put out or content, I grinned. I was betting on the latter.

"His name's Poco," she said, though I already knew that. Poco's ears twitched, but he didn't look up. "It's short for Apocalypse."

When I looked at her, she shrugged. "Isn't that what this is? Anyway, I found him a few weeks ago. Or more like he found me. Saved me from a group of those things. Flesh eaters," she sneered. "That's what the news called 'em. I hate that name. He can't be turned, ya know." I didn't know that, but she didn't seem to care if I answered or not "He's been bitten a few times fighting 'em," she continued.

Not that the conversation wasn't fascinating, but I'd been on edge since we'd left the convenience store. I needed answers. *"You shot that man."* Though I'd signed carefully, I still winced as the movements pulled at my wound.

She gave me an apologetic look. "I have no idea what you said. Sorry. Oh, wait!" Jumping to her feet, she went to rummage around inside the van, coming back with a small notebook and pen.

"Found these in the glove box. Knew they'd be useful," she said as she handed them to me.

The notebook was unused and the pen worked after a quick scribble, then I wrote down my question. She watched, nodding.

"Yeah, I shot him," she answered without remorse.

She read my next question and sighed. Picking up a piece of gravel, she rolled it between her fingers before throwing it away. "I followed you."

But how? I hadn't seen another vehicle on the road.

Reading my mind, she grinned shyly. "You didn't even

see me, did you? I stayed back far enough so you wouldn't. Though I admit, I lost you. If you hadn't broken down, it would have been hell finding you again."

Before I could finish writing my next question, she answered. "While you guys were swimming in the river, I took a peek at the map that guy was carrying around. The quiet one?"

When I raised an eyebrow, she continued. "I was hiding in the woods when you and those guys found that barn. I've been hanging around ever since." She sighed again and leaned back against the van. "I thought about coming forward. Sucks being alone, ya know? And there were three of you, which I thought meant there might be room for one more. At first, I stayed back to make sure it was safe. Two guys and one girl. Wasn't sure if they were holding you against your will. Wasn't long before I realized that wasn't the case at all." A light pink flushed her cheeks. "I promise I'm not a peeping Tom. I didn't, like, watch or anything."

Her cheeks turned a bright red and I almost felt bad for her. I was more amused than anything.

"Anyway, it kinda looked like I'd be the fourth wheel, which sounds pretty even if you don't take into account yall's relationship. So, I hung back. Glad I didn't completely disappear, though. That asshole on the mountain was one nasty piece of work," she said, biting out the last few words.

I patted her hand then wrote, "thank you."

"Oh, you're welcome," she grinned. "Us girls have to stick together, right?" Her smile vanished. "So, I missed a lot of what happened at the cabin, but I did see your friend. I'm sorry he was bitten. What made you leave without 'em?"

Closing my eyes, I hung my head and took a deep breath through my nose. I'd done well to not think about Kaden or Mason since I'd left them, and now that the subject had been brought up, my eyes stung with suppressed tears.

"I'm sorry I brought it up," she whispered. "How about we get back on the road, and you can tell me about 'em when you're ready." Her voice turned uncertain. "That is if you're okay with me tagging along."

Snorting, I rubbed at my eyes with one hand as I wrote my answer with the other.

The girl's hand went to her chest in mock hurt. "I would not follow you anyway, thank ya very much!" Then she laughed. "Well, maybe I would."

"By the way, my name's Annabelle Price."

I shook her outstretched hand, then scribbled down my own name.

Her grin widened. "Nice to meet you, Jane Thornton. I promise not to get ya killed if you promise me the same."

"Deal," I wrote. Then I narrowed my eyes. *"How old are you?"*

Standing, she brushed off the back of her pants and gave me a wink. "Older than ya think."

All three of us climbed back into the van. This time, I drove. Annabelle and I had both agreed it would be easier for her to give me directions. She chattered the entire time about nothing in particular, jumping from one subject to another while I listened quietly. I didn't mind. And it was easy to figure out that Annabelle had missed having someone to talk to. I'd also found out that my assessment of her age had been way off. I'd never met a twenty-three-year-old who looked so young before. According to her, that happened all the time. When her nose scrunched up in disapproval, I could see why. It was adorable.

"There!" Annabelle pointed to a small opening in the trees. Hitting the brakes, I took the turn sharply, sending Poco an apologetic look in the rear-view mirror when he whined.

"Sorry," Annabelle said. "I almost didn't see it.

We climbed the winding one lane road, up the mountain at a crawl, for more than an hour before our progress was halted by a locked metal gate that took up the entire width of the road. After a quick assessment, we decided to hike the rest of the way, and luckily for us, we didn't have to go far.

"Wow," Annabelle whispered.

The breath flew out of my lungs when we first walked into the clearing. The house was remarkable, with its stone façade and white front porch. It was like walking back in time.

"Look!" Annabelle pointed to the overgrown garden. "And there's pens already built for livestock."

It was obvious that no one lived here any longer. There were no animals in the pens, the garden was full of weeds, and there was an overall sense of emptiness I picked up from the house. Still, we were careful as we let Poco inside to check the place out first. When he gave a small woof to indicate the all clear, Annabelle squeezed my arm excitedly.

"We could make this a home," she whispered. Then she gave me a big grin before heading inside the house, her exclamations of wonder followed.

Home. Gripping the porch railing, I looked out over the property, listening to the distant sound of water either from a creek or a river nearby. It was like a piece of heaven sitting smack dab in the middle of hell.

I closed my eyes, my grip on the railing tightening until my injured palm throbbed. How could I make a home here? Without *them*?

Gritting my teeth, I looked out of over the property once more. This was a gift. Neither Mason nor Kaden were forced to give me this. Yet they had. And I would accept it gratefully. Not only for them, but for me. And Annabelle.

So, how could I make a home here? Without them? I could, and I would, because that's what I had to do to survive.

"JANE. JANE, HONEY, IT'S TIME TO GET UP."

With a pounding heart, my eyelids fluttered open at the familiar voice. A voice I'd painfully missed and would never hear again outside of my dreams. Which was how I realized immediately that I was dreaming. A dream I knew all too well. Though the warm, feminine voice had sounded as if it'd been spoken right next to my ear, it had actually come from downstairs in the kitchen.

I climbed from the bed, shivering as cold air swept across my skin, and hurried to the stairs. The peeling floral wallpaper blurred in my peripheral vision causing me confusion. Instead of the oak from my childhood home, cream paint coated the wooden railing beneath my fingertips and a glance at my bare feet on uncarpeted stairs showed me why I felt so cold. This wasn't my old house. This was the home me and Annabelle were living in.

The location of the dream had changed, but would the rest? Would the owner of the voice be here?

One of my questions was answered when I found my mother, her back to me, humming a meaningless tune as she stood in front of the stove. Internally, I sighed with relief that at least that part of the dream had not changed. This was the only portion I looked forward to every night. A chance to see her again.

Her long silver hair had been pulled into a neat bun at the nape of her neck. She'd gone prematurely gray in her late twenties, and I had a clear memory of her threatening to dye it on many occasions, but my father would beg her not to, telling her how much he loved it just the way it was. She'd blush, slapping his arm as if he were joking. But she had never used a single drop of dye. Not even after he'd passed.

"Jane. Are you ready?" she asked without turning away from the stove.

This part of the dream was a memory. It had been the first day at my new job. I wasn't sure why my brain had decided to put that particular conversation on repeat. There'd been nothing special about it—only the same discussion I'd had with her several times over the course of my life.

Instead of answering, I watched her, my anxiety growing as she asked me questions. *Where would I eat lunch? When would I be home?* It wasn't that I didn't want to answer them, it was that I couldn't. I was just an observer in this dream. But I soaked in her presence…her voice…because I knew this dream would take a turn for the worse. Already, the cold seeped into my bones. I could see my breath in front of my face as the temperature dropped.

"Don't be upset with her. She only wants what's best for you."

I turned to my father who sat at the dining room table reading a newspaper. His skin was pale and his lips were tinged blue. By now his sandy-colored hair should have been streaked with gray, but he'd still been young when he died. I'd only been eight years old at the time.

His words had been out of context, but it was something I'd heard him say many times during my childhood.

I wanted to go to him, or at the very least stare at him a little longer. But I had no control of my body, and my heart twisted with sorrow as my head turned away. My eyes were immediately drawn to the window where a shadowing figure hovered on the other side of the back door. I sucked in a shaky breath, knowing exactly what was about to happen.

"No," I tried to say, but it only sounded in my head. There was nothing I could do to stop my mother as she opened the back door.

"Well, hello, John," she greeted our neighbor, then gasped as they both fell to the floor in a tangle of arms and legs. John's face was hidden in the crease of my mom's neck, his fingers gripping tightly to her arms as he fed.

This was the scene that would repeatedly play over and over in my mind. She didn't scream. She never screamed. It would be over too quick for that.

I trembled, my body weeping in my sleep as I watched my mother being murdered. The life in her terrified gaze dimmed. It would be over soon. This was the end of it. But as the dream lingered longer than usual, I began to panic for another reason. I should have woken up by now.

Just as the thought crossed my mind, another change happened. The flesh eater pinning my mother to the floor stopped feeding. His head lifted slowly and he sniffed the room as if sensing my presence. My already racing heart picked up speed, bursting with adrenaline as he turned his head in my direction. Would I experience the same fate as my mother? Would he attack while I stood paralyzed? I would have preferred that outcome. Instead, I woke with the image of Mason's dead, milky eyes staring back at me.

Heart galloping, I stared at the ceiling, willing my body to still its trembling and my lungs to take a decent breath. I hadn't woken up so shaken in a long time. I shivered at the memory of my ex-lover's face, his mouth covered in my mother's blood.

I climbed from the bed before I could think more about it. It was just a dream. A dream that wasn't even close to reality. For one, Mason wasn't the one who'd killed my mother. And two, Kaden would have never allowed Mason to turn.

A rush of sadness swallowed me whole. Mason was surely dead by now. It had been weeks since I'd left them. And underneath the grief was also another kind of heartache. Kaden had never come.

After throwing on a pair of jeans, I laced up my boots and headed for the stairs. Halfway down I heard first the sizzle, then the smell of bacon frying in the kitchen. Grinning, I flew down the stairs to reach my newest friend. We had decided to take turns making supply runs, while the other would stay to protect the farm. She'd been gone for three days. I'd known as time went on we'd have to venture farther out than the closest town if we were going to find anything, but it hadn't stopped me from worrying.

"Hey, sleepy head," she said as I rounded the corner.

Five or six candles dotted the table and counter where she worked. Which made me wonder how I was smelling bacon. The stove was hooked to a portable generator. The refrigerator, however, was not.

With her back to me, Annabelle stood in front of the stove, her hips moving side to side as she hummed under her breath a song I'd never heard before. The scene was too much like my dream, causing my stomach to tighten uncomfortably.

"Hey, you okay?" Giving me a concerned look over her shoulder, she turned off the burner and waited.

Instead of answering Annabelle's question, I asked, *"Bacon?"* Her lessons on sign language had been going well, but she was still a little unaccustomed. It could take years for her to become fluent.

Under the table, Poco's tail thumped impatiently against the hardwood floor. Smiling, I bent down to rub behind his ears, receiving doggy kisses on my cheek in return.

"Huh? Oh, no. Canned ham," Annabelle corrected. Holding up the plate, she sent me a wry smile before setting it down on the table next to me. "I got a case of the stuff. It's been a while, but I remember it tasting almost like bacon if you sliced it thin and pan seared it until it gets crispy."

I wasn't so sure about that but I was willing to give it a try. It had to be better than the cold, gelatinous stuff. Sitting down, we both reached for a slice and took identical hesitant bites. I chewed slowly, thoughtfully. It wasn't quite as crispy as I expected. A little chewy.

"Hmm," Annabelle nodded. "Not bad," she said, giving a slice to Poco.

Not bacon. But close enough. And I'd been right. Much better than right out of the can. Before reaching for another piece, I asked where she got our breakfast. That's some luck running across a case of anything. Much less something like canned ham that would last for almost forever.

After watching my hands carefully, Annabelle's face broke out into a wide grin. "I found a few more generators." She waved a hand toward the mud room where three brand new generators were sitting.

I smiled back, ecstatic. We needed at least one more for the well-pump. It was going to be a chore to figure out how to connect it but I was willing to sacrifice the time and frustration. Hauling buckets into the house had gotten old.

I also made a mental note for our next supply run. We were going to need more fuel. So far, we'd been using gasoline. It was pretty easy to find, especially with so many abandoned cars everywhere. But it wouldn't last forever. We would need to come up with an alternative soon.

"I also found people."

Startled by her statement, I choked on the piece of ham I was trying to swallow.

Annabelle jumped from her seat, holding out a bottle of water. "Hey, you okay?" she asked.

Taking the bottle from her hand, I took small sips until my throat cleared, then wasted no time demanding answers. My hands flew as I hounded her for more information. *"Where are these people? Are they close? Are you okay? Did they hurt you? Where are they now?"*

"Jane, take a deep breath and calm down. I can't understand a thing you're signing. And your face is turning red."

I dropped my fisted hands on the table. *Calm down?* This was serious. Did she have any idea what could happen if someone found us here? Sucking in a breath through my nose, my teeth ground together as I glared at my friend. What had she been thinking?

Annabelle held out both hands, "Okay, okay. Just hear me out."

I nodded once for her to continue. This had better be good.

Instead, she stood from the table. "On the way in, I noticed a piece of the fence needs fixin'. Want to help me? We can talk while we work. I think the walk will do us good."

It took several deep breaths before I was calm enough to think clearly. The way Annabelle had eyed me warily, I could tell my reaction had surprised her, and I didn't like it. She deserved better. I decided to give her the benefit of the doubt and followed her outside.

With each step, the ground crunched beneath our feet as we made our way toward the tree line. The knee-high grass had turned dry and brown and the trees surrounding the clearing where the house sat were bare. Poco ran ahead of us, darting from spot to spot, sniffing his territory for intruders.

Overhead, heavy gray clouds walled up the sky. Snow was coming. It wouldn't be our first snowfall of the season, but we'd had it easy so far. Winter had just begun, and things were bound to get worse. I looked forward to spring. As soon as the ground thawed, we could start a garden.

As we ventured into the woods, Annabelle was unusually quiet. I wanted to ask her again about the people she'd met, but I shoved my gloved fists into my coat pockets and stared straight ahead. I was older than her by only three years. Not old enough to mother the poor woman. At times, I couldn't help it. Though only twenty-six, I sometimes felt like a hundred and twenty-six.

My anxiety began creeping to nuclear levels. If she hadn't spoken by the time we reached the fence, I would ask her again. Annabelle could take care of herself. She was smart, strong, and resourceful. Everything you needed to be in this world. But we were partners now. We had to be able to communicate if we were going to survive.

The bare trees made it easy to see the fence about thirty yards ahead of us. When we'd first walked the property, and found it to be surrounded by a seven-foot-tall chain link fence with brown plastic inserts, we were surprised and relieved. I didn't know why Mason's uncle had decided to protect his property so heavily, but I was grateful. Neither of us knew exactly how large the property was, maybe three or four acres at least. We walked it regularly, looking for damage to the fence or anything out of place.

Not only were we well-protected here, the stove used gas instead of electricity, and there was a working generator. We used it sparingly, though. Also, in the basement, we found jarred food that would definitely come in handy this winter, as well as some root vegetables that looked good. Mason's uncle must have been preparing. And recently. The vegetables looked fairly fresh and the jars only had a light covering of dust on their lids. But where had he gone? My teeth nibbled on my lower lip. I wished I would have asked Mason about him. I wished I'd asked Mason a lot of things.

Annabelle sighed, catching my attention. She wore the same black leather coat she always wore with her arrows hanging from her back in a black quiver that blended with her coat. She carried her bow in her hand at her side. My eyes narrowed disapprovingly at her bare hands. She never wore gloves. I'd tried a billion times to tell her it was getting too cold to spend hours outside without them, but she'd claimed she couldn't shoot well with them. I'd let it go for the time being. But in a month, it was going to be too cold to go without. Unless she wanted to lose a finger or two.

"They were nice," Annabelle said, breaking the silence.

My heart thudded as I looked up to meet her wary eyes.

"I promise, it's not that bad. I saw a group of four, three men and one woman, coming out of a grocery store I was about to check out. I hid and watched them as they loaded up two SUVs with supplies. Then I followed them." She shrugged. "I figured they probably emptied the store anyway."

Head shaking from side to side, I stared at my friend like she was nuts. Had it ever occurred to her to just run away when she saw them? Of, course not. This was Annabelle I was talking about. *Follow them?!* I scoffed. How had this woman survived this long?

"And they caught me."

I stopped walking, my eyes widening at her revelation. I immediately began scanning her for injuries, but she looked the same as always. *"Are you okay?"* I signed.

Holding her arms out, she smiled. "Jane, I'm fine. Promise. They were totally cool. They took me to their place. It's huge, Jane!" She said excitedly. "It's like a little town or something. They built a big wall around an apartment complex. It's a really neat setup."

None of what she'd said so far lessened my anxiety. In fact, it only caused my heart to pound even harder. She hadn't just found a few people. She'd found a huge *group* of them.

"They asked me questions, but I promise, I didn't tell them where we were. They were cool. They gave me the ham and said they'd like to start trading with us. See? Perfect set up. We could help each other."

My heart rate slowed, but I still wasn't convinced that this group was as perfect as she'd claimed.

"I showed a couple of people how to shoot." She held up her bow. "Easy."

I let out the breath I was holding. *"This is too dangerous. What if they hurt you?"*

Even if it was possible Annabelle understood that lengthy sign, she didn't see my question, too busy staring at the fence.

Her face pinched in confusion. "Huh. I could have sworn the fence was bent right here."

I looked up and down the fence line but didn't see anything other than a few places where the plastic inserts had cracked or chipped off. Nothing of concern there. *"Wrong place?"* I signed.

She shook her head. "No, look." Bending down she gripped the chain link at the bottom and gave the fence a little shake. It didn't move.

Crouching next to her, I peered at the spot she was pointing at. You could definitely see where the metal had been bent - it still curved slightly in - but it had put pushed back in place and one zip tie held two links together at the very bottom. From the look of it, the hole wouldn't have been big enough for a person to get through. That wasn't what had both Annabelle and me looking at each other, a hint of fear in both our eyes.

"Who fixed our fence?" Annabelle asked the question I had been thinking.

Angry barks and growls erupted from somewhere in the distance causing us both to jump to our feet.

Poco!

———

C.E. BLACK

is a Maggie Award Winning Author in Paranormal Romance. She self-published her first book in 2011 and has since published several novels, novellas, and short stories in the Paranormal, Fantasy, and Sci-Fi Romance genres. Though steamy romance, hunky heroes, and feisty heroines are C.E.'s specialty, she enjoys surprising her readers with action-filled plots and exciting twists that make for a fast-paced read.

Her official website is www.ceblack.org.

www.ingramcontent.com/pod-product-compliance
Lightning Source LLC
Chambersburg PA
CBHW022035170626
46808CB00003B/1216